"What are you looking for?"

Spencer smiled. "I'm looking for a bride-to-be, Ms. Ryerson."

Sudden relief flooded Kate. She held up her left hand. "I'm afraid I'm already taken."

"Exactly," he said with a twinkle in his eye. "What I should have said is that I'm not looking for a real bride, just a pretend bride-to-be, a short-term companion, if you will. I'm not looking to form a romantic attachment. So you, Ms. Ryerson, are perfect."

Kate curled her left hand into a fist, as if the truth would come crashing down and her ring slide from her finger, exposing her. He looked like a prince in a book of fairy tales, the very stuff that girlish fantasies were made of. A smile that could make a woman want to share all of her secret desires.

"I don't think this is a very good idea," she finally said. "You don't even know me."

"We'll get to know each other well enough for what I have in mind," he assured her.

Dear Reader,

Ring in the holidays with Silhouette Romance! Did you know our books make terrific stocking stuffers? What a wonderful way to remind your friends and family of the power of love!

This month, everyone is in store for some extraspecial goodies. Diana Palmer treats us to her LONG, TALL TEXANS title, *Lionhearted* (#1631), in which the last Hart bachelor ties the knot in time for the holidays. And Sandra Steffen wraps up THE COLTONS series about the secret Comanche branch, with *The Wolf's Surrender* (#1630). Don't miss the grand family reunion to find out how your favorite Coltons are doing!

Then, discover if an orphan's wish for a family—and snow on Christmas—comes true in Cara Colter's heartfelt *Guess Who's Coming for Christmas?* (#1632). Meanwhile, wedding bells are the last thing on school nurse Kate Ryerson's mind—or so she thinks—in Myrna Mackenzie's lively romp, *The Billionaire Borrows a Bride* (#1634).

And don't miss the latest from popular Romance authors Valerie Parv and Donna Clayton. Valerie Parv brings us her mesmerizing tale, *The Marquis and the Mother-To-Be* (#1633), part of THE CARRAMER LEGACY in which Prince Henry's heirs discover the perils of love! And Donna Clayton is full of shocking surprises with *The Doctor's Pregnant Proposal* (#1635), the second in THE THUNDER CLAN series about a family of proud, passionate people.

We promise more exciting new titles in the coming year. Make it your New Year's resolution to read them all!

Happy reading!

Mary-Theresa Hussey

Mary-Theresa Hussey
Senior Editor

Please address questions and book requests to:
Silhouette Reader Service
U.S.: 3010 Walden Ave., P.O. Box 1325, Buffalo, NY 14269
Canadian: P.O. Box 609, Fort Erie, Ont. L2A 5X3

The Billionaire
Borrows a Bride

Myrna
Mackenzie

SILHOUETTE Romance®

Published by Silhouette Books

America's Publisher of Contemporary Romance

SILHOUETTE BOOKS

ISBN 0-373-19634-2

THE BILLIONAIRE BORROWS A BRIDE

Copyright © 2002 by Myrna Topol

All rights reserved. Except for use in any review, the reproduction
or utilization of this work in whole or in part in any form by any
electronic, mechanical or other means, now known or hereafter
invented, including xerography, photocopying and recording, or in
any information storage or retrieval system, is forbidden without
the written permission of the editorial office, Silhouette Books,
300 East 42nd Street, New York, NY 10017 U.S.A.

All characters in this book have no existence outside the imagination of
the author and have no relation whatsoever to anyone bearing the same
name or names. They are not even distantly inspired by any individual
known or unknown to the author, and all incidents are pure invention.

This edition published by arrangement with Harlequin Books S.A.

® and TM are trademarks of Harlequin Books S.A., used under license.
Trademarks indicated with ® are registered in the United States Patent
and Trademark Office, the Canadian Trade Marks Office and in other
countries.

Visit Silhouette at www.eHarlequin.com

Printed in U.S.A.

Books by Myrna Mackenzie

Silhouette Romance

The Baby Wish #1046
The Daddy List #1090
Babies and a Blue-Eyed Man #1182
The Secret Groom #1225
The Scandalous Return of
  Jake Walker #1256
Prince Charming's Return #1361
Simon Says... Marry Me! #1429
At the Billionaire's Bidding #1442
Contractually His #1454
The Billionaire Is Back #1520
Blind-Date Bride #1526
A Very Special Delivery #1540
Bought by the Billionaire #1610
The Billionaire's Bargain #1622
The Billionaire Borrows a Bride #1634

*The Wedding Auction

Silhouette Books

Montana Mavericks
Just Pretending

Lone Star Country Club
Her Sweet Talkin' Man

MYRNA MACKENZIE,

winner of the Holt Medallion honoring outstanding literary talent, believes that there are many unsung heroes and heroines living among us, and she loves to write about such people. She tries to inject her characters with humor, loyalty and honor, and after many years of writing she is still thrilled to be able to say that she makes her living by daydreaming. Myrna lives with her husband and two sons in the suburbs of Chicago. During the summer she likes to take long walks, and during cold Chicago winters she likes to *think* about taking long walks (or dream of summers in Maine). Readers may write to Myrna at P.O. Box 225, LaGrange, IL 60525, or they may visit her online at www.myrnamackenzie.com.

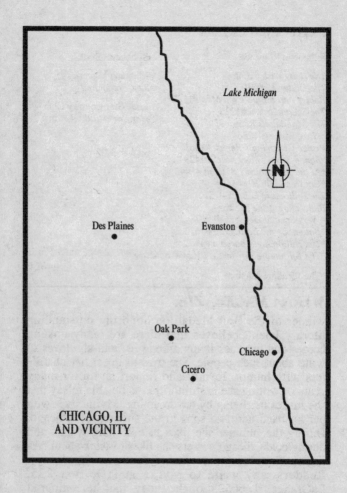

Lake Michigan

N

Des Plaines

Evanston

Oak Park

Chicago

Cicero

CHICAGO, IL
AND VICINITY

Chapter One

"Well, gentlemen, I think I may have found the perfect lady to help me work my miracle." Spencer Fairfield held out a brochure and gestured toward a woman who was heading toward the risers at the First Annual Suburban Chicago Job Auction for Charity.

"Hmm, very nice in a girl-next-door way, but do you really think anyone will believe that you're dating her? She's not your usual style, Spence, is she?" his friend Ethan asked. "Are you sure you can pull this off?"

"I wasn't referring to her looks," Spencer said, eyeing the dark brown hair and trim figure of the woman in question and admitting that Ethan was more than right about her appearance. There was something fresh and untouched about her. And no, she wasn't his style at all, but then, he wasn't looking for his style today, was he?

"I know something about this woman's character," he said, holding out the piece of paper. "If this brochure is correct about who she is and where she came from, then I knew her once. A long time ago."

"Uh-oh. Old girlfriend. Not good to hire them. Especially for something like this," his friend Dylan warned.

Spencer chuckled at his friend's concern. He watched as Kate Ryerson stepped up to the stage, her mist-green dress sliding against her curves as she moved. Very subtle and lovely curves, too, he couldn't help noticing.

A frown drew his eyebrows together. He wasn't supposed to notice such things. At least not about these women. He wasn't here to find a playmate.

"Kate's not an old girlfriend," he said. "Well, I suppose she did once tell me that we were going to get married. I was seven at the time. She was six."

"Definitely a mistake to hire her, then," Ethan mused. "She might sue you for breach of promise."

But that wasn't even a remote possibility, Spencer thought as Kate Ryerson's gaze raked the audience, paused on him for a millisecond, and then moved on. She didn't recognize him. He doubted she would even remember his name.

"Won't happen," he assured his friends. "I don't intend to bring up the past. Her mother was our maid for the summer. She brought Kate with her because she couldn't afford a sitter, and the two of us occasionally entertained each other. I doubt the lady wants to resume playing house with me. Especially since it says here," he noted, holding out the brochure, "that she's engaged to be married."

"Well, in that case, she can't very well show up at your grandmother's house party and pretend to be your date, can she?" Dylan asked. "Could get incredibly confusing and messy. Besides, who would believe the two of you were romantically involved? As Ethan said, she's not the type you favor, and everyone will know that.''

Spencer kept his eyes on the woman on the stage. As his friends had pointed out, he usually dated tall, willowy, chesty blondes with sultry blue eyes and pouty lips. Kate was slender, but she was petite with small, delicate breasts, a direct gaze that hid nothing and promised nothing and she moved with purpose, not an attempt to seduce. She looked very...practical. She certainly didn't look like the women he took to his bed.

''She *would* elicit some intriguing questions,'' he mused.

But then she stared out at the crowd and he forgot all about those questions. She swallowed delicately, her nostrils flared ever so slightly, and he could tell that she was a bit nervous. Well, who could blame her? He and his friends were examining her as if she were the last appetizer on the plate, and if they were ogling her, then so were others. He wondered if her fiancé was here and how he felt about her being the sudden object of every man's attention.

Spencer glanced around the audience, but all he saw were admiring stares and a few smiles. No man looking as if he wanted to tear cold, unyielding steel with his teeth.

Kate stepped forward, throwing her shoulders back as if she were preparing herself for battle. Her breasts might be small, but they looked delicious. Or would, once a man peeled back the cotton that covered her, Spencer thought, frowning again.

Apparently he wasn't the only person who thought

so. "I think I'm in love, sweetheart," some drunken man in the back called loudly.

Kate turned a delicate pink, she took a slight step back, then raised her chin and stepped forward again. She glanced toward the auctioneer. "Mind if I say a few things, Donnie?"

The man smiled at her. "Say all the things you like, hon. Take your time, too. No rush."

When she finally smiled and nodded, her dark brown hair brushed against her jaw. A pair of dimples came out of hiding. Spencer nearly groaned. He'd forgotten. Kate's dimples were the only frivolous thing about her. At six, they'd been cute. At twenty-nine, they were, he conceded, deadly.

"I just wanted to let everyone know that I'm a school nurse, and I've gotten a chance to meet and work with some of the kids at Safe House, the charity this auction benefits. They're good kids, but they're endangered, living in some of the rougher areas of the city where drugs and gangs are prevalent. We've helped some of them over the years, but there are always more to help. They're children, you know. A truly worthwhile cause. They need us. We have to do something. That's why I'm here. That's the only reason why I'm here."

When she made that last statement, her hands were firmly planted on her hips. Spencer smiled. Even though he hadn't known Kate well, even though they'd only been children, and twenty-three years had gone by since he'd last seen her, that was the one pose he wouldn't forget. Kate was very firm on what she wanted and didn't want and what she would and wouldn't do.

That might be a problem if he decided to hire her.

"Spencer," Dylan said, near his shoulder. "Think, man. Carefully. You and Ethan and I have been best friends since college. We know you well, and your family knows you even better. Has it occurred to you that they are going to be suspicious if you bring someone so very different from the ladies they're used to seeing you with?"

"I never bring ladies to my family gatherings."

"No, but your picture is in the paper with alarming regularity."

True, and the blonde standing just to the left of the stage was very much like the women who usually appeared in those pictures with him, a beauty with an extraordinary body.

"Yes, the leggy blonde," Ethan remarked, seeing where Spencer was looking. "Now, *she* looks like your classic type."

"I agree, she's a bit more believable. She's the type I'm drawn to as a rule, but that's the problem, isn't it? There's a reason I don't invite the women I consort with to my family gatherings, and it's because what's between us is strictly short-term. Bringing one of my…dates to a family affair would be misleading, even cruel, if any woman should take that as a signal that I was interested in something serious. Besides, staying true to type isn't going to relieve my grandmother's anxiety. She's a very smart lady." And her anxiety was getting worse the older he—and she—got. He was worried about her more than he wanted to admit. She was making herself frantic over his continued single and emotionally uninvolved state, fussing herself into illness and doing desperate things. He meant to relieve her mind, even if he had to hide the truth from her.

"Kate looks like a woman a man might choose for a wife," he said simply. "The fact that she already belongs to someone else makes her perfect, because I'm not willing to risk any romantic complications." Fairfields had a duty to marry and reproduce eventually, but those who had the bad judgment and misfortune to fall in love tended to fall so hard that that love ended up destroying significant parts of their souls. It had happened to his father. It had happened to his grandmother. It wasn't going to happen to him.

"Kate may be safe, but she looks like true marriage material," he insisted. "She'll pass the test."

Ethan studied her. "Perhaps. There certainly seem to be plenty of men here who look like they'd willingly turn over a new leaf and go down on one knee for her, and her fiancé no doubt feels that way."

The thought of the fiancé, the man who eventually *was* going to have Kate, the man who had a true claim to her time, gave Spencer pause for a second, but he quickly cleared his mind.

He warmed to his topic. "Her very difference from my usual 'type' will make her more convincing. Definitely a woman a man chooses for his home." Although he could imagine her in a bed as well, with her hair tangled and those incredible dimples telling a man he was welcome to sample her body.

"A definite air of domesticity," Dylan conceded, cutting into Spencer's most improper thoughts.

"She's perfect for this task," Spencer concluded. "My grandmother will take one look at her and relax. She'll be able to enjoy her birthday for once. And maybe she'll be less stressed and nervous and that will keep her much healthier. At least with Kate already taken, there won't be any possible complications."

He turned to Ethan and Dylan who were gazing at him with slow smiles as if he'd just said something incredibly amusing.

"Of course. No problems," Ethan agreed. "If you say so."

Spencer frowned. "What could go wrong?"

"I don't know. I think it's those hands on her hips and those eyes. Brown, aren't they?" Dylan asked.

"Green," Spencer answered automatically. "And don't worry about the hands on her hips. It means Kate isn't going to take any nonsense, from me or anyone else. If she decides to do this, she'll go full steam ahead."

"There's the catch," Dylan and Ethan said, almost as if they shared the same brain.

"*If* she agrees," Ethan clarified.

"A practical woman wouldn't get involved in such a harebrained scheme, would she?" Dylan asked.

Good question, Spencer agreed, but it didn't matter. He looked down at the brochure and saw the words *engaged* flashing before his eyes. That alone made Kate perfect.

"I'll just have to be convincing," he said with a smile and a shrug. "Now go lay claim to the ladies you've already hired for your own impossible tasks," he told them. "Let me worry about my lady and my problem. I'll handle the complications."

"*If* you manage to hire her. She's a nurse. Could be in great demand," Ethan said.

His friend was right, Spencer realized as Ethan and Dylan left, and he turned to find that the bidding had begun. Several men in the audience were already battling over Kate.

"Too bad. She's meant for me," he whispered.

Kate slipped her hands into the folds of her skirt to keep anyone from noticing that her fingers were trembling. She hated putting herself on display this way, but heck, she'd meant every word she'd said about Safe House. Those kids were more important than her fears. Still, her fears were very real. They were being fueled by that tall lean man with the golden-brown hair and the soot-gray suit that cost more than her entire wardrobe. A dream man, most women would say.

The worst kind of man for a woman like her.

Dreams were dangerous. Reality was so much better. Safer. Ryerson women were known for being suckers for dreams that took over their lives and ruined their worlds. Fortunately, she was the one Ryerson who had successfully bucked tradition. She wasn't going to risk failure now.

Still, it was difficult to ignore a man so gorgeous. Especially when he was examining her as if he knew just what she looked like when she slipped beneath the sheets at night.

Her breath caught in her throat, her cheeks felt unaccountably warm. Completely irresponsible to be imagining such things. She looked away and tried to concentrate on her reason for being here as Donnie read her qualifications.

"Please let a woman hire me," she whispered beneath her breath. Not that she hadn't had successful work relationships with men before. Just not lately. She didn't want to deal with the possible complications. Of course, if a man did hire her, she could always pull out her fiancé, Kate thought, fingering the plain gold band on her left hand.

Not for real, of course. Her fiancé didn't really exist, but no one needed to know that. He served a purpose. He insulated her from her own weaknesses and the weaknesses of men that she didn't want to encourage.

So let a woman hire me, she thought. Or if it's a man, then let it be one who's old and fatherly or one who absolutely adores his wife.

But fervent thought just wasn't enough, because thirty seconds into the bidding, the golden-brown-haired man glanced up at her and then moved nearer the stage.

"Fifteen thousand dollars," the man said in a deep quiet voice. His lazy smile had half the women in the audience turning their attention from the auction block to the man.

Kate's nerves felt as if they were trembling as much as her hands. But she'd learned from years of nursing that a steady expression and a take-no-prisoners tone of voice could work wonders with most people.

"Excuse me, sir, but you don't look like you need a nurse," she said, staring directly into eyes that could convince the most chaste woman to shimmy out of her underwear.

"You don't look like most nurses I've met," he said with a glance that sent a delicious wicked shiver straight down through her body. Kate took a deep breath to chase away her reaction. The man was obviously used to getting his way with women.

"We don't have to wear white or the funny little

hats anymore,'' she said. ''Just because I'm not dressed for the part doesn't mean I'm not a nurse.''

''And just because a person's wounds aren't visible doesn't mean they aren't there,'' he answered softly.

Touché. She knew that better than anyone. She nodded. ''You're right. I'm sorry. You do need a nurse, then?''

He shook his head slowly. ''Not at all.''

Uh-oh. What did he need, then?

''Excuse me, some of us are here for the auction,'' a man's cranky voice called, and the auctioneer nodded.

''Sorry, Kate, he's right. Place your bid then, man,'' Donnie told the complainer.

''I don't want to bid on her. Not when he's zapped things up to fifteen thousand,'' the man said, nodding toward Kate's highest bidder so far.

Donnie looked around. ''Anyone bid more than fifteen thousand?''

Kate knew it was too much to hope for, but she also knew that working for that gorgeous man with the velvet voice and the I-can-make-you-sigh eyes was just going to be a nightmare. And he'd already admitted that he didn't need a nurse.

''Going once,'' Donnie said.

Kate felt an urge to plead with the audience, to name off her qualifications all over again, to stress what an asset she would be for a family or a sweet little old lady.

Of course she didn't, and when she stole a glance at her bidder, she thought she saw sympathy in his gaze.

''Going twice,'' Donnie said.

The man might have felt sympathy, but he didn't withdraw his bid.

"Sold to the man in the gray suit," Donnie said.

Kate took a deep breath. So be it. She had been hired. She was a professional. She would do whatever job this man had hired her for, so long as it was respectable. And if it wasn't respectable, the charity would ask him to leave.

This wouldn't be so bad, she supposed. After all, it was only summer work. A few weeks at best. She was probably just being silly. There was nothing to be nervous about.

Slowly she came halfway down the risers as her new employer stepped up until she was only one stair above him. Still, she had to tip her head back slightly to stare into his eyes. He was close enough that she could breathe in the scent of musk and soap and man. His shoulders were so broad that she could not see past him on either side.

"I don't understand," she said tentatively. "You said you didn't really need a nurse, but that was an awful lot of money to bid."

He nodded slowly, almost kindly, she thought for half a crazy second. Which was silly. The man had been looking at her as if she was a choice bit of goods he intended to buy. He had hired her to do some task, and she had more or less agreed to that task by simply showing up here today. This was business. Cut-and-dried, no need for kindness.

"I didn't lie. I don't need a nurse. And I bid a great deal because I can and because I'm going to ask a great deal of you. More than you may feel comfortable giving."

Kate's heart began to pound fast. She knew that

her eyes had probably grown alarmingly large. She just hoped that she didn't look frightened. As a nurse, she'd learned to disguise fear even when fear was justified, but this was a different kind of fear than she was used to.

"What…what are you looking for?"

He smiled then, and yes, his smile was kind. "I'm looking for a bride-to-be, Ms. Ryerson."

Sudden relief flooded her soul. There was still time to head back to the stage and try again. She held up her left hand. "I'm afraid I'm already taken."

"Exactly," he said with a twinkle in his eyes. "What I should have said is that I'm not looking for a real bride, just a pretend bride-to-be, a short-term companion, if you will. But not in any real sense. I don't want to lead any woman down a false path and let her believe that I'm looking to form a romantic attachment. I'm not, so you, Ms. Ryerson, are perfect. You're already in love with someone else. Someone else already loves you. You're exactly what I need right now."

Kate curled her left hand into a fist, as if the truth might come crashing down and her ring slide from her finger, exposing her. She didn't want to pretend to be romantically involved with this man. Doing so could prove very dangerous to a woman's sense of reality. She was sure of it.

He looked like a prince in a book of fairy tales, and she could not allow anything into her life that held a hint of impossible dreams coming true. Those types of emotions could be so very destructive. She had seen it, she had lived it and she had gone to the edge herself a time or two.

"I don't think this is a very good idea," she said.

"Oh yes. I think this is a very good idea, Kate."

"You don't even know me." And for a second she thought he *did* actually blink. Well, why not? She'd been told many times that her direct approach to life messed with a man's style.

"We'll get to know each other well enough for what I have in mind," he assured her. "Allow me to introduce myself. I'm Spencer Fairfield."

And Kate knew that the hand she slipped into his was icy against his warmth. Spencer Fairfield. She knew the name, though he no doubt would have forgotten hers years ago. And now she also knew just how impossible this situation was.

Spencer Fairfield was the very stuff that girlish fantasies were made of, the fantasies she'd given up years ago. Looking into his eyes, she could see that in some ways he hadn't changed. Those were eyes that could make a woman dream. That was a smile that could make a woman want to open up and share all her secret desires.

If she allowed herself secret desires—which she didn't.

If she took this job with this man, she would spend all her time fighting the inclination to brush up against him like a cat shamelessly begging for cream.

"I'm afraid that this job will require that you be on hand around the clock for the next week," he was saying. "And some travel. We'll be visiting my family at my grandmother's estate on Lake Geneva."

Not far. Only a couple of hours' drive north, but…

Suddenly Kate felt a sense of relief—and maybe just a hint of loss—rush through her.

"I'm afraid that might prove to be a bit of a problem,'' she said, ''if you need me to travel and visit with your family. You see, I have a baby, Mr. Fairfield. I guess I'm not the woman you're looking for, after all.''

Chapter Two

Spencer felt the jolt go through him. She had a baby? For a moment, disappointment slid through him. He wasn't sure he wanted to examine the details of that disappointment. Was the baby her fiancé's or some other man's? Had she been married before? Obviously, more had been happening in Kate's life than just getting engaged.

And no doubt part of his disappointment had something to do with having his perfect arrangement snatched from his fingers.

"I'm sorry to pry, but…is the baby's father part of your life?"

She blinked as if he'd hit her. She raised her chin in what seemed almost a defiant gesture. "He's long gone. Toby was my sister's child. She died soon after his birth and his father didn't stick around."

There was definitely anger in her voice. And perhaps a touch of sadness.

"I'm sorry, Kate."

She shook her head. "Don't be. I miss Ruth. I wish she'd lived, but I don't regret Toby. He's my world."

And the baby was hers alone. Maybe this perfect arrangement might still be salvaged.

"My grandmother loves babies," he said, half to himself.

"Pardon me?"

"This trip is to celebrate her birthday. It's a tradition, an annual pilgrimage to the original Fairfield estate. My younger brother, myself, various aunts and uncles, a few grown cousins. No babies, though, not in a great many years."

He smiled gently, noting that this could be a good thing. Apparently Kate wasn't in agreement. Her green eyes were wide, a trace of panic rising in their depths. "Well, then, I wouldn't want to spring Toby on your grandmother," she said. "At eighteen months old he can be a handful. Noisy at times, of course. Disruptive to a household that isn't used to babies."

Kate was warming to her subject now, Spencer couldn't help noting. She really didn't want to go with him on this trip. Not that he could blame her. This was a completely crazy situation, especially for a woman who liked to keep both feet firmly affixed to the ground. Besides, her life was here—and so was her fiancé.

But, Spencer reminded himself, he was looking for someone to help him reassure his grandmother and give her peace of mind when she was frantic with the belief that he might never marry—or at least that he might never marry while she was still around to witness the union. Maybe he'd just found the perfect woman to ease his grandmother's mind. If that was true, he wasn't going to give up so easily.

"Kate, Fairfield House was practically made for babies," he said. "Lawns that stretch on forever, a nursery with all the amenities. My grandmother never gets rid of anything and she always keeps her home in perfect shape. Since her greatest desire is for my brother and myself to marry and give her great-grandchildren, everything is still ready for a baby even though there are no babies. And if there's anything else that your son needs, anything that's missing, we'll bring it in."

His voice dropped low on his last words and Kate took a step back, her heel catching against the step of the risers. Spencer slid his hands around her waist to keep her from falling, and for a minute they stood there, his hands spanning her waist, her softness warm and pliant beneath his fingers. He could feel her panic as her breath caught.

She moved slightly, her body sliding beneath his touch, and a punch of desire hit him hard.

Carefully he let her go.

"I'm sorry, but I don't understand," she said. "Why would you want to do this?"

He couldn't help smiling, because she was right. This plan sounded insane. "Kate, my grandmother is a wonderful woman, the only woman I've had as mother for many years. But she's growing older, frailer, and now, at a time when I only want to bring her happiness, I'm causing her to worry. I'm thirty and I'm not married or even engaged. In my grandmother's world, that's serious cause for alarm. Every Fairfield in the past century has married before that age and married for love, to boot. Some, my grandmother included, believe that every Fairfield has a soul mate, and she's concerned that I might never find mine if I don't get busy. So, for the past few years, when I've shown up for her birthday, she's invited a companion to keep me company. I always explain the situation to the young woman. I'm there to visit my grandmother, not to form an attachment and claim my bride.

"At the best of times, it's uncomfortable. At the worst, it's downright unpleasant, but regardless of which it turns out to be, my grandmother always ends up more worried when the week is over than she was when I arrived. This year I intend for things to be different. I'm going to bring my own companion. My grandmother won't spend the week hoping we'll hit it off, she'll already be confident that things are heading in the right direction. For once she'll be able to enjoy her own birthday bash. I want her healthy, not worried."

"That's nice. I like that. I take it you don't believe that Fairfields truly have soul mates."

He shrugged. "Maybe some do, but that doesn't necessarily result in happiness. Having one person holding your future in his or her hands can be and has been devastating for some. The Fairfield Curse. I will marry someday, I do need an heir, but it won't be that way, not for love. I've known women who've been devastated by a man who cannot return their love. In my own family I've seen what the Fairfield Curse has to offer, and it's a fate I'd never pursue."

She nodded. "I understand, and I wish I could have helped you, but…"

"You have a baby."

"Yes." She nodded.

"So bring your baby. We'll keep him safe, I promise."

She took a deep breath. For half a second, he thought that she was going to say yes. But then she looked full into his face. Something in those lovely green eyes flickered. He had a serious urge to lean closer to her, to touch her. As if she sensed that, she tightened her lips.

And he knew he was going to lose the battle.

He hated losing.

Especially *this* battle.

Turning to one side, Spencer looked toward the auctioneer, who had moved on to the next employee and the next. A lull ensued as he waited for the next woman to climb the steps.

"Excuse me," Spencer called.

Donnie looked up.

"I'd like to raise my bid to thirty thousand," Spencer said in a deep voice that carried.

"But you've already won her."

Apparently not. "I'd like to donate more, then." Spencer felt Kate stiffen beside him. Her fingers touched his sleeve.

"You don't have to do this," she whispered.

He looked down at her. "You're mad about this cause," he said. "I want you to be mad about mine. And I can well afford to donate more to needy children. The ones at Safe House and yours."

"Are you trying to bribe me?"

"Absolutely. It doesn't appear to be working. I can donate more."

"Are you sure this is for your grandmother?"

He couldn't help smiling. "I'll make sure you get references before we leave."

She nodded. "She's very special, then?"

"I think you'll agree once you meet her."

"But you're lying to her."

He shook his head. "Not really. I'm not going to claim that you and I are actually engaged. I'm just going to show up with you and let her draw her own conclusions. I know Grandmother Fairfield. She'll draw them and she'll be ecstatic that I'm finally 'fulfilling my destiny,' as she calls it." He grinned at that.

Miraculously she grinned back.

"Will you come with me, then?" he asked. "I'll provide you with all the information, references and reassurances you need. I'll even speak to your fiancé if you like."

She drew in a deep breath. "No. I…I'd prefer to do that myself."

Ah, so the man would be jealous. And why not? Spencer thought, looking down at Kate. She might not be the type of woman he usually chose, but she was very appealing in her pale green dress with her sweet green eyes and her dimples. A vision, really. If he wanted to make her his forever, he'd certainly take exception to some man spiriting her away so that she could act the part of lover for a week.

"You'll come, then?" He held out his hand. He waited.

Kate eyed Spencer's hand, the fingers long and strong. It was so tempting to simply reach out and say yes, but she needed to think and she couldn't think clearly at all if she was touching him.

He'd certainly pushed the right buttons when he'd talked about his grandmother's estate being a great place for her son. She'd never taken Toby anywhere, and even though he was just a baby, she wanted to take him places, to show him off, to get him out of her too-small apartment where the landlord threatened to throw her out every other month because she had a baby and he didn't like babies.

And then there was her new boss who was imagining himself in love with her. In spite of her ring, he still pursued her. He was the reason she'd invented the phony fiancé, and maybe he saw through her subterfuge, but she didn't think so. Her boss simply seemed to find her even more appealing since she'd become "engaged" and on the verge of becoming permanently unattainable. He'd even called her after the school year had ended.

That made Kate angry. She needed her job, and getting involved with the man who held her career in his hands wasn't an option, even if she had wanted to, which she didn't. The stress was eating her up inside.

Right now all she wanted to do was to take her son and get away from every problem and every temptation in the world. Including Spencer Fairfield.

But the darn man had gone and donated fifteen thousand more dollars to Safe House. That money would do so much good for kids who really needed a break. What was she supposed to say?

A yes would mean she'd be with Spencer for an entire week and that was daunting. Even as a boy, he'd been appealing. He had inspired her to make up fairy stories when she was beginning to be old enough to realize the danger of such things. As a man, what could he inspire a woman to do?

Something reckless, no doubt about it.

"Kate?"

She looked into his eyes. She couldn't answer. Something about the way her name slipped off Spencer's tongue told her that staying with him would be a very bad idea, indeed. She should walk away and spend the next week the way she spent every week, trying to keep Toby from making too much noise and annoying the landlord.

But shouldn't a child as young as Toby be allowed to make a bit of noise, to express his delight without having his mother shush him constantly? It broke her heart to do that.

And what could a week hurt? How much could happen?

A lot, she thought, but she tried to block the truth. And the best way to block one thought was to replace it with another. She looked up into Spencer's mesmerizing blue eyes. "When do we leave?"

Spencer took her hand. As his skin touched hers, her heart started pounding.

"Just as soon as we can collect your things and your baby and tell your fiancé. I'm going to love dating a woman who is already engaged," he teased.

Uh-oh, she thought, but she managed a weak smile. Spencer need never know. After all, they were only going to know each other for one week of their lives.

Which was very good, because she was already enjoying his touch far more than was wise.

Three hours later, Spencer showed up in front of Kate's apartment building in a gold stretch limo.

She blinked when she answered the door and peered out at the car. "A limo?"

He shrugged. "It's what I do. Fairfield Enterprises produces custom-fit limousines. What else would I transport a lady in? And you needn't feel uncomfortable. This one is relatively simple."

But when Spencer opened the rear door so that

Kate could place Toby and his car seat inside, she turned and placed her hands on her hips. "Simple?"

"It's not that large."

"It has a diaper-changing table, a refrigerator, an automatic bottle warmer, baby blankets and toys."

He held out his hands. "Some of my clients need these things. *You* need these things, Kate," he said softly, looking toward her son, who was looking around with bright blue eyes, his chubby cheeks creased in a grin. "See, your son approves."

She wrinkled her nose at Toby and gave him a hug. "Traitor," she said, unable to keep the love from her voice. "He's young and easy to influence."

"He's young and he needs certain amenities," Spencer argued. "I happen to have them available. Why not use what I can offer?"

His voice was so low that for a second Kate thought that he was offering something other than a luxury limo. But when she looked up at him, he had a devilish look in his eyes. He was teasing her, daring her.

She was sure her cheeks were pink, but she managed to lift her chin. "Very practical," she agreed in a dry tone. "But where's the mobile to keep him entertained in case he gets cranky or bored?" She opened her eyes wide and tipped up her chin, letting him know that two could play at the teasing game.

With a grin, Spencer reached inside and pressed a button. Automatically a panel opened in the roof of the car and down dropped a trio of blue and pink ponies chasing each other in a circle. He pressed another button and a lilting lullaby began to play. "There's a video screen," he noted, "and a full complement of appropriate fare. Teletubbies?" he offered.

She rolled her eyes, but couldn't restrain her own smile. "I think we're good for now," she said. "In you go, pumpkin." And she stepped in to fasten a babbling Toby into his car seat. She started to sit down next to her child, but Spencer placed his hand on her arm.

"Will he be all right back here by himself for a while, do you think? I suppose you and I should at least get to know a bit about each other before we reach our destination."

Of course. She couldn't very well show up at his grandmother's house and admit that the only things she knew about Spencer were those she'd discovered when she was six years old. She hardly thought that his grandmother would be impressed by the knowledge that Spencer thought most girls but her were "icky." She couldn't help smiling at that thought. Somehow she was pretty sure that this virile man didn't find girls icky at all anymore.

"Care to share what's delighted you so?" he asked.

She shook her head and climbed from the car to move into the front seat. "It was nothing," she said, and that was true. She had no intention of letting Spencer's grandmother know that she had ever met him, because she had no wish to remind Spencer of their past. For one thing it would be…well, deflating and sobering when he had to admit that, of course, he didn't remember the daughter of his mother's maid. But more than that, to remind Spencer of those days was to bring back a time when she hadn't completely given up her belief in the pot of gold at the end of the rainbow. For all intents and purposes, that girl should never have existed. There were certainly no traces of her remaining now. And that was just the way she wanted to keep things, Kate thought. No reminders that she had once been well on her way to being as big a doomed dreamer as her mother and sister. She was the only one left alive now. She had to be reasonable and smart and very practical if she was to survive and always be there to protect her son.

"What would you like to know?" she asked nervously after Spencer had helped her into the car and circled around to climb into the driver's seat.

"Well, I know you're a nurse. A school nurse?"

"Yes. At Edwards Elementary School. Mostly I deal in colds and fevers and the occasional sports injury. Lots of hand-holding with scared little munchkins who are feeling bad and missing their moms." She couldn't help smiling at that.

"It's important to have a good mom substitute when you're hurting," he agreed, "as well as someone who can fix you up."

Kate shrugged. "What else?"

He considered the question for a minute. "Family? Besides Toby? A former husband, perhaps?"

She fussed with the material of her skirt, pleating it with nervous fingers. "None. I've never been married. My mother died in a car accident when I was in college and as I mentioned, my sister died over a year ago. Now it's just Toby and myself."

He turned dark blue eyes on her. "I'm sorry. It must be difficult without your family."

It was, and yet her family had always been so dependent on her for everything. It had been difficult being a mother to your own mother. That didn't mean she missed her any less.

"Toby's my family," she said somewhat defensively, trying not to remember the fears that hit her in the night, the worry that she was all her child had. "How about yourself?" she asked. "It must be nice to have a large family."

He shrugged. "Most of the time. Sometimes they try to make my business theirs. Out of love, of course. Be forewarned."

She nodded.

"Is there anything I need to know about your fiancé?" he asked, his voice quiet in the very quiet car. "He's all right with all of this?"

Well, maybe if he were a real person, he wouldn't be, but...

"He's fine," Kate said, her voice a bit too clipped. "And what should I know about you?" she asked, rushing on.

Spencer laughed. "Besides the limo business? Well, you might need to know that my two best friends in the world also made...um, purchases at the auction. Dylan Valentine hired a very nice young woman, April Pruitt, to assist him in baby-sitting his twin half brothers while their mother is away, and Ethan Bennington hired Maggie Todd with the aim of turning her into royalty."

"Royalty?"

He chuckled. "You see, you and I have an easy task. We just have to convince everyone that I'm besotted with you and you with me."

Kate's pulse began to run, to race.

"I'll do my best," she said, taking a deep breath.

Suddenly Spencer slid his hand off the wheel. He took her fist in his gentle grasp, coaxing her to unfurl her fingers.

"Easy," he whispered. "Just be yourself, Kate. Don't work at it so hard."

Of course. If she frowned and stiffened up with resolve every time someone looked her way, they would soon know that her heart wasn't involved with Spencer.

But her heart *wasn't* involved with Spencer and she didn't want it to be.

"Will we have to...I don't know. Be intimate?" she asked, and his fingers suddenly tightened on her own. Carefully he released her.

"We'll be friendly," he said. "For starters."

Which left a whole lot of room for what came after the start, she couldn't help thinking. But she had committed herself to this. She would see it through.

"I'll be the perfect guest," she promised. "I won't give anyone reason to doubt my reason for being there."

He smiled then and Kate began to breathe a bit easier. Maybe just being a nice person, posing as a friend, would be enough.

But when they finally turned down the lane that led to Fairfield House, doubts assailed her. The driveway was long with elm trees spreading their branches low on both sides, like something out of a southern plantation. Lake Geneva was a popular retreat for wealthy Chicagoans, but the summer crowds were not in evidence here. This was completely private, very stately. Kate couldn't help feeling as if she had entered another world.

"Oh my."

Spencer chuckled. "My grandmother likes pomp and circumstance. She says that the Fairfields owe it to the world to put on a good show, to give back what we have, both in charity and in performance, which includes making sure everything looks good."

"Well, it all certainly looks good," Kate said, hoping she didn't sound too naive. When the car came out of the trees, the house stood before them a football field away on the top of a low grassy hill. Made of stone and wood, it looked as if it had almost as many rooms as her school had classrooms.

"It's a bit like a castle. I hadn't realized just how...I mean it's—"

"Ostentatious. I know, but it's what my grandmother wanted. My grandfather built it for her."

And if the woman was anything like the house, she was imposing, wealthy beyond words. Kate struggled to breathe normally.

"You'll do just fine, Kate," Spencer said quietly, as if he'd read her thoughts. He pulled up in front of the house and helped her out. He waited while she bent to remove Toby from the car.

Just at that moment, the front door opened. From her place on the far side of the car, leaning over her child, Kate looked up through the opposite window. She watched as an elegant, silver-haired woman stepped from the door.

"Spencer, love," she called, practically hopping from one foot to the other in spite of her age. "I thought you'd never get here. Come on, come on. I have a special surprise for you."

And a tall, blond amazon emerged from the house. She had honeyed curls and curves that weren't even slightly concealed by a formfitting beige dress.

"Here she is. Spencer, you remember Angela. She's the granddaughter of my old friend, Harriet Stoughton, a very good family, you know. And she's come all the way from California just to see you."

The woman smiled at Spencer, and Kate thought

she'd never seen such a beautiful creature in her life. Angela was the kind of woman most men would kill to date. And of good family too?

What on earth am I doing here? Kate thought as a slow, painful ache slipped through her. Embarrassment, of course. She didn't even know half her family. She'd never met her father at all. Suddenly, she was the fifth wheel, the maid's daughter all over again.

It was a part she knew how to play, but one she'd promised herself she didn't need to play anymore.

"I can take a cab home," she said softly, low enough so only Spencer could hear as she straightened and rose to her full height.

And she looked right into Spencer's blue eyes. Eyes filled with humor and challenge.

"Turning coward on me so soon, Kate?" he asked. "I think not. The fun is just beginning."

Chapter Three

For half a second, Spencer thought he saw a trace of anger in Kate's eyes. Good. He was a little angry himself. At himself.

He could have warned Kate what to expect and informed her that he was going through with his plans regardless of whatever woman had been provided for his entertainment this year.

He had to give his grandmother credit, though. She'd finally gotten desperate and given in. Angela was just the type he usually dated. The last two women had not been. So what would his grandmother and the assembled guests think of Kate?

No time like the present to find out.

But when he smiled at Kate, she was still frowning. "This is not going to make your grandmother happy," she whispered. "She has everything planned."

"So do I."

"That woman is supposed to be your date."

"A man likes to choose his own woman, Kate." And he thought he heard her breath catch in her throat. Good, she was off balance. That meant she wouldn't have time to be nervous.

"Let's go, Kate. Let's do this."

She blinked. "I don't know. You're sure?"

"Oh yes." He reached out for Toby.

She shook her head. "It's all right. I can carry him."

"And I'm sure you do just that all the time, but it makes more sense for me to carry him today. I'm bigger, and I can take him in one arm," he said, doing exactly that. "That leaves one arm free." And he took her hand. As they walked to the house, he tried not to notice how soft her skin was.

"Grandmother, it's so good to see you," he said, finally letting go of Kate and shifting Toby to his hip so he could hug the woman who'd taken on a mother's role for many years.

Loretta Fairfield hugged him tightly. "You've been working too hard. It's been weeks since I've seen you," she said. She pushed back and gazed down at Toby with wide, surprised eyes. Then she tried to peer around Spencer and get a glimpse of Kate.

He smiled to himself, knowing that curiosity was practically killing her.

"It's been much too long since I've seen you," he agreed. "Hello, Angela," he said politely. "It's always good to renew acquaintances with Grandmother's friends."

"I'm sure it is." But the woman was smiling as if she knew that he'd been through this before.

"I brought a guest myself this year, Grandmother. I was sure you wouldn't mind. This is Kate Ryerson,

a very special lady.'' And he reached out to take
Kate's hand and pull her forward. She was blushing,
her cheeks a delicate pink. Somehow he was sure that
she would rather be stitching up a bloody wound than
standing here by his side right now. His eyes nar-
rowed at the thought, but he didn't let go of her hand.

"Why—welcome, Kate,'' his grandmother said,
only her eyes betraying her surprise. She held out her
hands, ever the gracious hostess. ''I'm…well, I'm
guess I'm just flabbergasted, actually,'' she said.
''And delighted. Spencer's never brought a guest before, you know.'' Loretta's smile grew, it brightened,
she practically beamed, and Spencer knew that the
wheels were turning. She was thinking that he'd
found his soul mate at last.

A small hint of guilt nudged him for doing this to
her and to Kate. But he refused to give in to it. He
had brought Kate here as his personal guest. He
would see this through, and he would make no promises to anyone.

Kate glanced up at him once, as if to gauge what
her response should be, but then she quickly looked
away. ''Thank you for taking me in on such short
notice. I'm very honored to be here. You have a beautiful home.''

At that moment, Toby crowed. He began to buck
in Spencer's arms. Small though the child was, the
movement caught Spencer off guard, and he tightened
his grip on the little boy, afraid he might fall, but
Toby seemed fearless. He was reaching out, opening
and closing his little fists.

Spencer followed the invisible path from Toby to
his grandmother, and then he smiled. ''The star pin
you always wear in your hair, Grandmother,'' he said.

"It obviously fascinates him. His name is Toby, by the way. He's Kate's."

"Well, anyone can see that, Spencer. He's the image of her, and—well, he's not yours. Or is he?" she suddenly asked.

Kate's delicate pink blossomed into a deep rose. Already this situation was proving a trial for her. A trial for him, too, as a vision of himself carrying Kate to his bed lodged itself in his mind.

"Toby's just Kate's," he managed to choke out.

"Oh, I see." Was that actually disappointment in his grandmother's voice? Did she want him to have a child out of wedlock? He supposed she did. She wanted him to do anything if it was the result of a love match. He knew in his heart that what she wanted was to relive the love she'd once lost. And her means of doing that was to see that her grandsons had a great love of their own. He and Connor, however, weren't cooperating.

"May I hold your baby, Kate?" His grandmother turned to Kate, a childlike look of longing on her face. "He's so precious."

Kate looked happy—and helpless. "Yes. Yes, of course. If you truly don't mind," she said.

His grandmother chuckled. "If I don't mind," she repeated, as if it were a good joke. "Of course I don't mind. It's been years since I've held a baby." And she pulled the star pin from her hair and took Toby from Spencer. Immediately Toby quieted. The two of them gazed at each other as if they were both old souls getting to know each other.

"Let's get this young man inside and find some toys for him," she said, smiling down at the baby. "And while we're at it, we'll see if we can't locate

Connor and his girl, Bridget," she said, returning Toby to Spencer's arms.

Ah, so his grandmother *had* made provisions for his little brother as well.

"Come Kate, dear," she said as if she'd been saying that very thing all her life. And she disappeared into the house with Angela right behind her.

Kate started to step forward, but Spencer stilled her with a touch of his hand. "Are you all right?" he asked.

She glanced up at him, blinking as if dazed. "I think I'm fine. This just seems too easy. She didn't even question my being here."

He knew what she meant. His grandmother had clearly brought Angela for him, but had switched her allegiance to Kate without argument. It was what he'd wanted, and yet Kate was right. He felt sudden guilt for having neglected to settle down as his grandmother wished and more guilt at leading her astray today.

"I know. Perhaps it's wrong for me to imply that you're something you're not, but it's good to see her at least smiling and hopeful for a change. She frets about Connor and me."

"She loves you."

"Yes, more than we deserve."

"I suspect that a grandmother's love is as unconditional as a mother's love. Someday Toby may feel the same about me."

He smiled. "Will you set him up with buxom blondes?"

"Don't," Kate whispered urgently. "I feel sorry for Angela. This has to be uncomfortable for her. She was clearly brought here for your pleasure."

Her eyes were wide and luminous and questioning.

"Kate, I am not going to bed Angela while I'm here."

She blinked, and he realized that he had phrased that badly.

"I'm sure she *is* uncomfortable, though," he said softly. "I'll speak to her and explain the way things are."

"And what will you say?"

He smiled and wished that he felt free to stroke her cheek. She looked so lost and concerned, but she was like a wild creature who had been caught in human hands. She was afraid and unsure of her place here, and he knew that he would only make her nervous if he touched her in such an intimate way. "I'll merely let her know that my grandmother likes to bring enough males and females together so that everyone is partnered."

"But now she isn't partnered."

He let out a resigned breath. "Would you like me to call up a friend and ask him to come be with Angela?"

"I suppose that would only make things worse. This is a rather awkward situation though, isn't it?"

It was. More for her than for him. He was used to his grandmother's matchmaking antics and the contortions he and his brother put themselves through to avoid unnecessary complications.

"She'll have a nice vacation in a very exclusive home," he told her. "Grandmother always provides recreational activities, and if I know her, she's already busy thinking of some man she can bring in for Angela."

Kate watched him nervously. "I'm being silly, aren't I?"

He did stroke her cheek then. He couldn't help himself. "You're being kind. And caring." And then, because she was looking distressed at his touching and his tone, he added the words he knew she needed to hear. Truthful words. "You're also being practical. Don't worry, Kate. Things will be all right."

"You're correct, I suppose. We're here. Everything seems fine. What could happen?"

"Thank you," he whispered. "I want you to promise me that if you do ever feel uncomfortable, you'll come to me and let me know what's wrong. Let's have openness between ourselves at least," he said. "All right?"

She blinked, she sucked in her lip, but then she nodded slowly. "As much as I'm able."

And he thought he understood. She had her fiancé. Of course she would have some secrets that he wasn't privy to. Something slipped through him at that moment, something harsh and uncomfortable and biting, but he'd learned how to obliterate uncomfortable thoughts.

"This will end well," he said, and he led her inside.

"So my brother has finally succumbed." Connor Fairfield took Kate's hand as she sat next to him at the dinner table an hour later. "And not to the fair Angela."

He was a beautiful man, with lighter hair and darker eyes than Spencer's, but there was a trace of something bitter in his voice.

"I'll live, Connor," Angela said from her place

across the table and two seats down. The smile she gave him wasn't sweet.

His eyes turned cold as he looked at her. "I thought you might survive. After all, there are other men with money in the world."

For a second, Kate thought she saw a trace of hurt in Angela's eyes, but the woman quickly shook her head and turned her smile, a real one this time, on Kate.

"Your son is adorable," she said. "How old is he?"

"Eighteen months." Kate couldn't keep the gratitude from her voice.

"They're so cute at that age. I'd like a child," Angela said. "But you have to have a man for that."

And for a minute Kate thought Connor sat up straighter in his seat. He was probably thinking what she was thinking. A woman who looked like Angela could have had any man.

Kate absolutely could not stop herself from looking up across the table to where Spencer was seated.

He was staring straight at her, his dark blue eyes intense.

Against her will, against all the warnings her brain was offering, her heart speeded up.

Automatically she reached to twist at her ring.

"Oh my goodness, they're engaged!" Angela was out of her seat and around the table in two seconds flat. She was reaching for Kate's left hand.

Oh no! What had she done? She'd forgotten, that's what, and apparently so had Spencer.

"You're marrying him," Angela said, and there was a touch of longing in her own voice.

"There'll be others," Connor said. And there was both sympathy and anger in his voice.

Angela looked up and glared at him, but then she glanced down at Kate, who was frantically trying to think of the right thing to say.

Kate thought she just might be ill. She looked to Spencer who was staring at her ring as if it were fire on her hand. There was such fierceness in his gaze that she almost felt the heat. She knew that if that heat ever touched her, she would melt. She would do things a woman like her had no right doing.

"No, Spencer and I are not engaged." She almost shouted the words.

"Of course you're not," Spencer's grandmother said. "No grandson of mine would give a woman a ring with a diamond the size of a pinhead. Would you?" she demanded of her grandson.

He looked up at her for a second, then returned his glance to Kate. He stared at her, his eyes holding her in place with their deep intent. "If I gave a woman my ring, I would make sure that she was branded as mine," he said. "I'd give her the Fairfield emeralds, of course."

"Hmmph, I thought so," his grandmother said. "And Connor would give his bride-to-be the Fairfield sapphires," she said to Bridget, the frail, fair-haired young woman seated by her side, a woman looking at Connor as if he were the devil incarnate.

Connor smiled at Bridget. She cowered in her seat.

Angela chuckled, and Connor scowled at her.

These things registered in Kate's mind, but mostly she registered Spencer's displeasure and his heat. She really had no excuse for not having already removed the ring, except that it had offered her shelter for so long that it had almost become a part of her.

"The ring," she said, twisting it and trying to think of an explanation that would salvage the situation. "Well, I wear it because—" She supposed only the truth would do. There was really no reason to withhold it other than the fact that it provided her some measure of confidence, a feeling that she could use it as protection against the feeling that she was drowning whenever she looked at Spencer.

Of course, telling the truth about her fake fiancé was the thing to do.

"I wear it—" she began again.

Angela touched her hand. "It's a fine engagement ring. I suppose it reminds you of when you and your husband were dating and first in love," she said. "You can't have lost him that long ago if Toby is only eighteen months old."

Kate looked up at the woman, straight into eyes as clear as a lake, and she knew that Angela didn't have a clue why she was wearing a fake engagement ring, but the woman did know that it was an engagement and not a wedding ring, and she knew that something wasn't right with this scenario. It was the sisterhood of women against the Fairfield charm, she supposed. The woman was giving her an out if she wanted it.

But what could she say? That she was wearing a fake engagement ring as a hedge against her own emotions and against overly amorous men? How could she say that, when she had come here to pose as Spencer's companion? How would that look to his grandmother?

"It's a silly thing," Kate said, neither agreeing with nor denying Angela's lie. "I forgot that I was even wearing it. Of course, I should have removed it long ago.'' And she took it from her finger and placed it in the pocket of her skirt.

But Spencer's grandmother was looking worried now. In the space of moments she seemed to have shrunk. It was clear that none of her plans were working. Connor's young lady was frightened of his dark scowls, Angela was partnerless, and as for herself, she'd thrown confusion and doubt over her reason for being here with Spencer.

She felt as if her face was flaming. She looked up at Spencer and thought she saw concern in his eyes. He gave her a sympathetic smile, but the width of the table separated him from her. She couldn't whisper to him that she was sorry.

She wished the room would miraculously empty out. She wished she could go back to yesterday.

"Spencer likes to be at the helm at all times, he likes to be in charge. He doesn't make many mistakes," Connor's quiet voice whispered at her elbow. "But he's not a man who holds grudges when other people make them. He's also fair."

"I know that."

"He's not really angry."

"I know that, too. I think," she said, catching on. Connor might wear a cynical expression, he might resent this whole matchmaking charade that played out here every year, but he loved his brother deeply and he sensed her consternation. He was worried that something was happening here that would cause a rift between her and Spencer. "I just hate being the cause of so much concern. And attention," she admitted.

He chuckled at that, close to her ear, and Spencer frowned at them. "Well, get ready for more attention.

You were interesting before, but now you're positively fascinating. My grandmother loves romance and she loves mystery. You've provided her with both. She'll be more determined than ever to make sure that Spencer gives you the Fairfield emeralds before this week is done.''

Kate took a deep breath. Of course, that would never happen.

But when she looked up at Spencer, he was gazing at her intently. ''Grandmother, I hope you won't mind if Kate and I ask to be excused. We need some time alone,'' he said softly.

Kate knew that was a very bad idea, especially given Spencer's mood right now.

But his grandmother was smiling. Color was returning to her face. ''Of course, my dear. You young people need time to sort things out. Take all you want. I'll just watch the baby.''

Spencer moved around the table and took Kate's hand, his eyes never leaving hers.

''Come,'' he said, and as if her body had no will of its own, she rose. She thought she heard Angela sigh and Connor groan, but she couldn't be sure and she couldn't tear her stare from Spencer's.

She followed him up the long, winding staircase, aware that every eye in the room below was on them. At the top of the stairs, outside the first door, her room, Spencer stopped. He opened the door and waited until she had stepped over the threshold. Then, out of hearing range, but still in full view of the party below, he took her hand and turned her around to face him. He looked down at her, his blue eyes dark and demanding.

"I'm so sorry," she whispered. "I completely forgot that I was still wearing my ring."

He shook his head. "Understandable. It's become a part of you. It came from the man you're marrying, the man who'll share your future. Tell me about him," he demanded.

She took a deep, faltering breath. She wanted to look away but she couldn't and so she swallowed hard, nervously.

"Fitz?"

"If that's his name."

She nodded slightly. She felt faint. She'd told this story before, many times, with no hesitation. This time felt different. Wrong.

"His name is Fitz Manning. He's thirty-two years old, he's an engineer. He…he loves children. He wants us to have…"

Spencer was staring at her so intently that her throat went dry, closed up. She was here for a lie of sorts, but this was a worse lie. Spencer only wanted her to pose as a companion, which she was, more or less. Her lie about Fitz was a real one.

"He wants you to bear his children," Spencer finished.

She licked her lips. "Yes," she said, her voice hushed.

He breathed in deeply. "Of course. He would. Tell me, is your…is Fitz a very jealous man?"

This was a crucial question. She wanted to say yes, because Spencer was an honorable man. And a caring man. She was sure of that. He loved his grandmother so much that he was willing to go to great lengths to make her happy. If she said yes, he would not push her. He would keep things friendly and impersonal.

But she knew without a doubt that right now he needed her to say no.

It wasn't a choice really. A wise woman would answer in the affirmative. She had always been wise.

But she was also cognizant that Spencer had helped a great many children today with his money. And he was trying to make his grandmother's birthday a success. There was a terribly anxious and confused older woman downstairs who deserved one good day. Was that asking so much? Was the price he was asking so very high?

"Is he a jealous man, Kate?" Spencer asked again.

She took a deep breath, she closed her eyes briefly. When she opened them again, she swallowed hard. "No. No, Fitz isn't a jealous man."

"Good. I'm glad your fiancé is understanding, Kate, because we have an audience, a confused audience right now. I think we need to fix that, to show them that you and I are real. I know you're not ready for this, and I hope you won't be upset, but with the world watching, I'm going to kiss you."

And he rested his hands on the door frame above her head. He leaned forward and took her lips in a kiss that left no questions unanswered. If anyone below was looking, and she was sure that all of them were, she was no longer merely Spencer's companion. To any interested party, she was completely his.

Chapter Four

Kate sat up in bed the next morning and, immediately, she touched her fingers to her lips.

"Absurd," she said out loud in reaction to her waking thought that her lips must look very kissed. Swollen. Absolutely absurd when Spencer had barely touched her. He hadn't even placed his hands on her.

He hadn't had to. She'd stayed with him as his lips had roved over her own. She had the most awful feeling that she had actually leaned into him. She couldn't quite be sure. Kissing wasn't something she had a great deal of experience with. Certainly she'd never had a kiss make her dizzy and leave her trembling.

Until last night.

She touched her lips again, then climbed from the bed and moved to the mirror, leaning closer. Could anyone see? Could they tell what had gone through her mind when Spencer had teased her lips open and mated his mouth to hers?

Again. Touch me. Please. She closed her eyes at

the very thought. She groaned and sank onto the floor in a puddle of white nightgown and bare legs.

No, no, no. This was not going to happen. She wouldn't let it. She had a life, a good one, a real one. She wanted nothing to do with those dreams that made a woman dizzy and excited, irrational and completely blind to reality. And that was the way it always played out if your name was Ryerson.

"So be careful," she ordered herself, sitting up straight. "Be rational."

Right. That was her, the rational one. So what if Spencer knew how to kiss a woman? She'd known that when she met him.

And lots of other women knew it, too. He has to have kissed hundreds, she reminded herself. And no doubt made every one of them dizzy and desirous of more than just one kiss.

So that was that.

"Get on with things. You're here to do a job. The touching is just a part of that, kiddo. Remember that and don't go getting all dreamy-eyed and ridiculous on me."

Kate got to her feet. She checked on Toby who was still in his crib, his little lips puckered angelically in his sleep. Then, content that her child was safe, she showered and dressed in a pair of winter-white slacks and an emerald sweater.

All right, I'm as ready as I'll ever be. No more putting this off. She picked up the baby monitor's transmitter and clipped it onto her belt. Time to face a new day. And Spencer.

On the first floor, breakfast was being served buffet style in the dining room. Kate peered around the corner. No Spencer. Somehow she didn't quite feel the relief and elation she'd expected to feel.

A low feminine chuckle sounded near her elbow. "Did you think that being in a different setting would change my grandson's habits? I assure you that he's just as lazy about rising here as he is at home."

Kate felt her cheeks growing warm. How little she knew of the man. She wondered if it showed and if anyone would guess their secret. Not if she could help it, but she definitely needed to educate herself about the man sleeping upstairs.

A sudden vision of Spencer, all of him, naked and glorious sprawled in the sheets, his chestnut hair tousled against the pillow, crept into her imagination. Kate swallowed hard. She barely stopped herself from shutting her eyes.

"Well, sometimes a change in scenery messes with a person's natural rhythms," she said somewhat lamely. "Have you eaten already, Mrs. Fairfield?"

The lady patted Kate's hand. "Hours ago. I'm one of those crack-of-dawn types. Spencer gets his lazy habits from his grandfather." Her voice was laced with deep affection. "But you go ahead and eat and then we'll chat. And please, call me Grandmother Fairfield or Loretta. You and I shouldn't be so formal with each other."

The woman's smile was kindly. Kate instantly warmed to her and felt a trace of regret. She hoped the lady wouldn't be hurt when her dreams of Spencer's wedding didn't work out.

"I'd like to talk with you," Kate said, and found that it was the truth, even though there was danger in spending too much time with Loretta Fairfield. It wouldn't take much for the woman to discover just how little Kate knew of Spencer.

Her time with him had been short. She'd been infatuated with him when he was seven. Already he'd worn the air of command that he would need when he grew to be a man. But he hadn't balked when she'd shown herself to be a bit strong-minded, too. She had this awful memory of herself demanding that he marry her when they grew up. He'd smiled and raised that terribly expressive left brow as he'd told her that he didn't think that would be a problem. That was just about all she knew of his character, except that now that he was a man, he could make a woman's body ache with desire when he kissed her.

Kate sucked in a deep breath and hoped she wasn't doing something ridiculous like blushing.

"I'll be back as soon as I've eaten," she told Spencer's grandmother. If she was going to act as Spencer's companion, then perhaps she needed to learn something of the man.

Other than the way he kissed.

The sound of female laughter greeted Spencer when he left the dining room one hour later. His ears told him that one voice was his grandmother's. The tightening of his body told him that the other voice was Kate's.

He shouldn't have kissed her last night. Or at least he shouldn't have kissed her so thoroughly. A brief touch of the lips might have suited his purpose.

Unfortunately, his body had taken over once he'd gotten close to her. Leaning over her, with those luminous green eyes staring up at him so nervously, he'd wanted nothing more than to taste her to the fullest, to deepen the kiss until those lovely eyes shed their concern and glazed over with passion.

At least he'd somehow managed to keep his hands off her. If he'd taken her into his arms, there was no telling where he would have stopped. Or if he would have.

With his entire family watching, that might have been a problem. And with the lady's engaged state, it most certainly would have been a problem. For her. For her fiancé. For himself, if the truth were known. Playacting was one thing. Assaulting another man's intended was something else completely.

He was going to have to stay very alert and aware of his body's responses where Kate was concerned. Especially now that he knew that the mere sound of her laughter made him burn. Definitely, he would have to work on his control. Maybe it would have been better if he hadn't hired Kate and had simply given himself up to the lovely Angela.

At least he wouldn't be waking up with erotic fantasies about Kate or wondering why an engaged woman kissed like a complete and charming innocent.

Spencer shook his head at that ridiculous thought. Surely it had been his imagination that Kate had looked as if he'd just given her her first real kiss last night.

And surely he should just drop any thoughts he was having about trying to kiss her again anytime soon. Her fiancé was obviously a restrained man. And a restrained man wouldn't appreciate another man teaching his woman passion.

The very thought made Spencer's body hard. He had to stop and count to ten. To twenty. And then to thirty. Finally he was somewhat in control of his thoughts. He pushed open the study door and entered.

His grandmother and Kate looked up from the photo album they were perusing. Loretta was holding Toby on her lap. She looked more relaxed than he remembered seeing her in the past five years since his grandfather had passed away.

"Spencer, darling, I'm so glad you're here. I was just showing Kate the family pictures and regaling her with tales of your exploits as a young boy. You were such a happy baby. All of us were blissfully happy back then, when your mother and my Edwin were still around. You remember?"

"It was heaven," he agreed.

"Yes, but it all gets a bit fuzzy after that. After your mother died when you were ten, your father didn't bring you around nearly as much. I have so many blank spots in the photo album."

Because his father had completely fallen apart after his mother's death and had never recovered even half of what he'd been before.

His grandmother looked at him with sad, understanding eyes. "He loved her so completely, just as my Edwin loved me, dear."

He knew that. He even regretted it, which was something, he realized, that was a bit strange for a son to have to admit. That all-consuming love that his father had felt for his mother had almost killed him. A little less love and a bit more friendship might have been preferable in his opinion. But in his family, that wasn't the way things were done.

"I so hope that you have that kind of love someday, Spencer," his grandmother said, just as she'd said the words every year for the past few years.

But Kate didn't know that this was a ritual. She was looking as if she wanted to run from the room, as if she was being sucked in deeper and deeper every second.

"Grandmother," he said gently.

She shook her head and held up her hand. "Oh, I know you're not even engaged yet. Forgive me, Kate. I tend to jump ahead and skip some parts. And speaking of skipping some parts, I think you'd better take up the family history from here, Spencer darling. Up to the bits Kate already knows about, anyway."

Which was absolutely nothing. He smiled down at his grandmother and at Kate. "I'd be happy to fill Kate in on the Fairfields' black past," he said with a grin.

"Spencer," his grandmother admonished. "We do not have a black past. You'll be scaring Kate off."

But Kate was starting to smile now. He'd been right in thinking that she needed a bit of teasing to make her forget that his grandmother was determined to see them wed.

"I don't think that Kate scares easily," he said softly, holding out his hand. "She's a very brave lady."

He gazed into her eyes, and she took a deep breath. To his grandmother, it no doubt looked like a breath of anticipation from a woman who was about to spend some time alone with her lover. Only he and Kate knew that the woman was simply drawing up her courage for the ordeal of the masquerade.

She placed her hand in his, and he closed his fingers around her softness. His body began to hum with the pleasure of simply touching her.

"Is your history really black?" she tried to tease,

but her voice came out a bit choked and he was afraid that she could feel the desire rising in him.

"The blackest," he said.

She raised her chin. "I'm a nurse. I don't scare easily, you know. I'll want to know all the gory details. Especially the blood-and-guts part. Any Bluebeards in your closet?"

"Oh, I'm sure we can dig up a few appalling ancestors if that's what you're in the mood for."

He chuckled and turned to give his grandmother a reassuring look. Which was a good thing, since she was looking a bit worried.

"You young people," she said with a sigh. "I'll never understand you. Don't you bring her roses, Spencer? Or diamonds? Or write her love poems? Or serenade her?"

"Serenade?" He laughed. "Me? Only if you want to run her off, Grandmother."

"You don't sing?" Kate asked. And Spencer shook his head slightly, warning her not to ask too many questions in his grandmother's hearing.

"I've protected Kate from my worst habits," he told his grandmother. "And yes, sweetheart, I'm afraid I do forget and sing sometimes. Like a beagle."

"Oh yes, I'd forgotten," Loretta said with a chuckle. "Spencer does have the most awful baritone. But then, love doesn't pay much attention to such things, does it?"

He wouldn't know. Still, he had a strange desire to ask Kate if her fiancé sent her roses or diamonds or love notes. Or sang to her.

He blotted out the thought. "Why don't we leave Grandmother and Toby to their play," he suggested.

"Where are we going?"

He hadn't a clue.

"The library, I think," his grandmother answered. "Yes, definitely the library, Spencer. Please. We've been dreadfully remiss in giving Kate a tour of the house and, of course I'll show her around myself this afternoon, but she should see the library with you. It's where all the family history is kept."

And it was also a rather dark and cozy room, Spencer couldn't help thinking. He was sure that very thought had passed through his grandmother's mind.

But he bowed slightly to Kate and reached out for her hand. "The library it will be. If you want to unearth some family skeletons, that's where they'll most likely be."

"Very practical to keep all the skeletons in one place," she said with a smile. "And that's where we must go, I suppose. Thank you for suggesting it," she said, turning to his grandmother.

The lady waved her away. "Go. Have fun. Your son and I will get acquainted," she said as Kate leaned over to touch Toby's cheek. "Isn't he a fine, quiet young man, Spencer?"

Spencer gazed down at the baby's angelic blue eyes and dark curls against his grandmother's silver hair. Best to be careful here. He wouldn't want her getting too attached to Kate's child or to build up her hopes for a marriage when there wouldn't be one. But she was right about the little boy who smiled so sweetly with eyes that believed that the world would always be safe and happy. How trusting they were at that age. How sad that they ever had to meet with any sadness in their world.

"He's a gem," he said to his grandmother and to Kate.

"He's a real baby," Kate said softly. "He cries and sometimes he's cranky. I love him to death, of course, but he isn't perfect. It wouldn't be practical for a child to be good all the time or to be expected to be consistently sweet. That's not reality, and I definitely want him to learn about reality."

Interesting. He wondered where that thought process came from. The Kate he'd known as a child had been very real but dreams had still counted. She'd obviously done a lot of living between then and now. A lot of hurting, too, he reminded himself. For over a year she and Toby had been alone.

Except for the fiancé, he reminded himself. He wondered if he or some other man was the reason Kate had gone from a no-nonsense six-year-old who, nevertheless, had dreams for the future, to a no-nonsense woman who wanted even a child to keep his feet firmly on the ground and planted in reality. But, of course, none of that was his business.

"That's a very practical viewpoint," he said.

"It's the way we live. Are you sure you don't mind watching Toby, Grandmother Fairfield?" she asked.

"It's a rare pleasure. Go on now, dear. I won't spoil him too badly while you're gone."

Kate nodded. "Thank you, but I confess to spoiling him myself now and then. It's a temptation. I'm ready now," she said to Spencer.

He tugged on her hand gently, and she moved with him. He allowed himself three seconds of savoring her nearness before he forced his mind down other paths.

"Ah, here we are," he said less than a minute later when he pushed back the heavy mahogany door to the library. "Lots of family ghosts in here." He indicated the paintings that covered and guarded one wall of the room. "An imposing lot, aren't they? Rather stodgy for the most part."

She smiled. "You're very proud of your family, aren't you? For all of your teasing, this room means something to you, doesn't it?"

He shrugged. "Well, I have to admit that it was rather daunting to come here as a child and realize that a whole collection of your ancestors was staring down at you when you were simply trying to locate a book, or hide, but yes, there is something very satisfying about being able to look up and relate the history of those who've come before you."

She nodded and her smile held, but there was a trace of something vulnerable in her expression. Again he was reminded that she'd lost most of her family.

"This is probably pretty boring stuff, anyway," he said. "Perhaps you'd rather see the gardens. Or the ballroom."

"I'd love to see both of those places. But this first, please. It must be very intriguing to be able to trace your family's history back through generations."

Which meant that she couldn't do that. He really was going to have to discover more about his charming companion. And not just because of this damn silly situation. He had the feeling that Kate Ryerson was an interesting person in her own right. Besides, he liked to know something of the people he hired, he reminded himself. That was the reason for the interest.

"I was quizzed on family history when I was a boy," he admitted. "My grandfather would bring me in here and spin tales about these people living on this wall. I believe that he fabricated some of the stories, especially the more scandalous ones, just to tease my grandmother, but maybe not all.''

"So there is a bit of scandal in the Fairfield family?" Kate's smile challenged him to come up with something outrageous even if he had to follow in his grandfather's footsteps and resort to fantasy.

"Well, I suppose we aren't completely stodgy. My family has a reputation for being rather single-minded when it comes to matters of the heart. One of my illustrious ancestors, Hamilton Fairfield," he said, indicating the stiff, dark-haired man's likeness, "left his wife for a dancer because he felt that he had finally found the one woman in the world for him. It created quite a stir at the time.''

She glanced up at him. "Ah, even you disapprove. I can hear it in your voice.''

"From all accounts he had a perfectly amicable relationship with his wife even if there was no great passion. I'm not one to believe in the family myths about love, and even if I were, I wouldn't approve. The man was a dreamer and a blackguard.''

"So there are no dancers in your future?"

He chuckled. "I didn't say that, but if I married a woman, I wouldn't go looking for some utopian love. I wouldn't leave a wife for a pie-in-the-sky love affair.''

She nodded. "Your grandmother believes in love. You must cause her a great deal of worry.''

"I'm afraid so.''

She smiled at that. "You're a very practical man, Mr. Fairfield. I like that.''

And her smile sent a jolt through him. A quite unacceptable jolt. "Shall we explore the rest of the library or do you want to hear more of the family history?''

''Oh, history first, please. They're such fascinating paintings. And all in pairs. Husbands and wives?''

''Mostly.''

''So…the lady next to Hamilton, is she—''

''She's the dancer. My great-great-great-grand-mother.''

''She's stunning. And her eyes are so…so luminous and almost…I don't know. Defenseless, maybe.''

''Yes. I've been told that my great-great-great-grandfather stood behind the artist the whole time he was painting. She was looking at him.''

Kate's eyes met his and for a minute he thought he saw a trace of panic in their depths, but instantly the look was gone. He must have been mistaken. The woman was, after all, a nurse. Panic wouldn't be a part of her nature.

''I wouldn't want to be like that, to feel like that or to let anyone see me like that,'' she said softly.

He understood completely. He approved, although a small part of him felt strangely aggrieved by her attitude. Total nonsense, of course. And he gave himself a mental pat on the back for hiring such an eminently practical woman.

She turned to the side, and he realized that he had been staring at her for long seconds.

''Could we see the rest of the room now?'' she asked.

''My family has always revered books. My grandmother especially. So she's divided the room into different areas to match the mood of the person who's reading. This section is for someone who has some serious work to do." He indicated an area of straight-backed chairs upholstered in leather, an ample desk with writing materials and a series of tall dark bookcases filled with reference materials.

"This other section is dedicated to those times when you're in the mood for some serious reading material," he said, waving toward the main part of the room, which consisted of plush sofas and easy chairs in hunter green and shelves of leather-bound classics.

"And this must be for those days when you simply need a bit of escapism," Kate said, moving toward a sunny alcove filled with overstuffed chairs and genre fiction. "What a wonderful room. A bit overwhelming for us mere mortals who don't have house-size rooms filled with books, but wonderful nonetheless."

"The world needs mere mortals, Kate. You shouldn't let this house overwhelm you. You're a nurse. You have more than rooms filled with books. You have the ability to change lives."

She grinned at that. "I'm a school nurse, Spencer. I'm not operating on people and saving lives."

He frowned. "You make an impact. A child who gets ill at school has to be frightened. You soothe, you make a difference in that child's life. And I would think that most parents would feel relieved to know that you're there at a time when they can't be. That's life-changing. It certainly gives your students a positive, less frightening view of the medical profession. If I had a child, I'd certainly be happy to know that he or she would be in your care if illness should strike."

Kate smiled up at him. "Did you say that your

family made great lovers or that they were all diplomats?''

He chuckled. "Is there a difference?''

She rolled her eyes. "Maybe not. At any rate, I thank you for showing me this room. I can see why your grandmother wanted me to see it. All this history.'' She indicated a small table on which more framed miniatures of Spencer's relatives were displayed.

"Not everyone enjoys looking at someone else's family portraits. I seem to recall someone once telling me that if they had their way, they'd have lots of pictures of cats and dogs on their walls.''

Spencer smiled and then froze when he saw the look of distress in Kate's eyes. He hadn't meant to bring up that long-ago past or to let her know that they had a prior connection. He supposed it was simply a response to the warm feeling and the teasing these past few moments had brought out.

Kate blinked and took a visible breath. "So you remember me, too. In that case, it's safe to say that I recall someone who once told me that he wanted to be a professional baseball player,'' she said dryly.

Spencer looked down into wide green eyes. Kate had her hands on her hips, daring him to bring up one more embarrassing thing from her childhood.

"Touché, Kate. And of course I remember you. We were friends.''

She turned her back and started toward the door. "We were friends. And there's nothing wrong with pictures of cats and dogs, you know. If they're done tastefully,'' she said, and he could hear the laughter in her voice.

"Oh, definitely," he agreed. "Especially on velvet."

Her shoulders began to shake and he reached out to turn her and found that her face had crumpled with laughter. "Oh, that was mean of you to bring that up," she said.

"Not mean," he said, shaking his head. "You were a charming six-year-old."

"But I'm not six anymore, Spencer."

No, she wasn't. She was a woman. Even through the cotton of her sweater, her skin was warm beneath his fingers, and she was engaged to be married to a man who would soon have the right to peel back her clothing and taste all that warm, soft skin.

He stared into her eyes for long seconds. Then he forced himself to release her.

A blush covered her throat and climbed up to kiss her cheeks. "Thank you for the tour," she said. "I can see why your grandmother wanted your...companion to see the family portraits. They're striking."

He shook his head. "She didn't really want you to see the family portraits. She wanted me to take you here because she thought it would be a good place for seduction."

"Seduction?" Kate's eyes widened in confusion.

Slowly Spencer grasped her chin between his thumb and forefinger and gently turned her to face the dark alcoves and corners of the rooms.

"Lots of soft couches and dark, quiet areas. She wants to make sure my lady and I have plenty of opportunities to fall in love. I'm sure she expects you to emerge from this room looking thoroughly kissed. I'm also reasonably certain she'll be watching."

Kate lowered her lashes. He could almost hear her

mind working when she took a deep breath, pulled her shoulders back and looked up at him. Slowly she lifted her hands to muss her hair. She reached up and unfastened the first button on her blouse.

He swallowed hard.

"Do I...do I look thoroughly kissed now?" she whispered.

She looked like someone he shouldn't be standing so close to for fear that he would lose control and take this relationship down paths it couldn't go.

"Not quite," he said, his voice coming out too husky. "A woman doesn't look thoroughly kissed until she's actually been kissed."

And he reached out and took her in his arms. His mouth descended to cover hers.

The soft, innocent touch of her lips turned him to fire. The taste of her burned deep and fueled his hunger. He wanted more than a taste, more than a touch. He wanted to claim her, to teach her, to slide inside her and mate his body to hers. And he would do that if he didn't stop now. When she left here she would look not only thoroughly kissed but thoroughly loved.

That wouldn't do. He forced himself to pull away.

"Now you look kissed," he managed to say.

And he reached for the door.

He wondered who was craftier, his grandmother or himself. Because while he had eluded her attempts to set him up with a date this year, she had had her way. He had never gotten involved with a woman on one of these family visits, but right now he was deep into lust for Kate Ryerson.

And that wouldn't do. She didn't want a relationship. She was engaged to another man.

But even that was a mystery. She kissed like a woman who had rarely experienced kisses.

What in the world did that mean? And did he really want to know the answer to that question?

Chapter Five

This was getting too complicated and uncomfortable, Kate thought the next morning as she snapped Toby into a white shirt and a tiny pair of bib overalls.

"You and I need to finish this up and get home, punkin, back where we belong," she said, smiling down at her son.

"Home," Toby agreed, kicking his feet. "Home, home, home."

"Exactly, and this place and any other place like it will never be home for people like us. We really don't belong here. I wish I hadn't agreed to this. Well no, that would be a lie. If I hadn't agreed to this, Safe House wouldn't be the grateful recipient of thirty thousand dollars. Still, I'm going to have to be careful from here on out. No more stupid stuff for Mom."

"Mom," the little boy said with a big smile. "You Mom."

"Yes, sweetheart, that's me. And it's the most important job in the world, the best I've ever had," she said, picking him up and holding his warm, baby powder-scented body close. "Who needs anything else when I've got you?" She certainly didn't need Spencer, that was for sure. The man was making her crazy with his kisses that made her forget that she was supposed to be an engaged woman. And he was making her feel guilty, too. She had made up her fiancé because her boss hadn't been able to take no for an answer, but Spencer wasn't interested in her in any personal sense. There wasn't any reason she could justify lying to him this way, especially when he was a good man, one who cared about people. The only reason she could possibly be hanging on to the charade of being engaged was that she didn't trust *herself* around Spencer.

Which was so true, she thought with a small groan. Every time he touched her, she practically forgot her own name. What must he be thinking when she, a supposedly engaged woman, seemed flustered by a simple kiss or two?

Probably that she was just like any other woman he'd ever met, which made her humiliating reaction to him all the more demeaning.

Kate sighed. She pushed her troublesome thoughts away and looked down into her son's big blue eyes. "I think you and I need some time to play. I've been neglecting you, my son, my heart. Want to spend the morning here with Mom?"

And away from Spencer.

She hugged Toby close, and he placed his chubby little fingers on her cheeks and gave her the baby kiss she desired. Kate breathed in his scent and wished that she and Toby could stay here together for the rest of the week. Alone. Safe. She wished that she had never met Spencer Fairfield.

"He remembered who I was," she whispered. "He remembers me the way I was." And that wasn't good. Even she didn't like to remember the way she had been as a child. A dreamer with no sense of self-preservation. A Ryerson, through and through.

But that girl was gone, and Kate wasn't going to allow her to return. Instead she would simply concentrate on getting through the next week as quickly as possible.

And maybe she and Spencer wouldn't have to touch anymore. Maybe now that they'd been witnessed kissing, simply giving each other longing looks would be enough.

Kate had not come downstairs yet this morning, and Spencer was pacing the floor. What was wrong? Was she sick? Was her son sick? Maybe she just needed some extra time.

His grandmother was beginning to give him sly smiles every time he made a turn of the room. In response, he sat down, picked up a newspaper and pretended to read.

"Kate must have been up late last night," his grandmother said softly. "Yesterday she was down at the crack of dawn."

"Maybe Toby had a restless night," he said from behind his newspaper. He read the same paragraph for the fifth time. The words didn't register.

"It must be hard raising a child alone," his grandmother said. "Kate could probably use a few hours to herself. Even a mother who loves her child to death needs to be alone at times."

And maybe she didn't want to come near him because he'd kissed her again when he really didn't have a good reason for doing so. That story he'd told about his grandmother expecting her to come out looking thoroughly kissed might have been true, but Kate's own efforts to muss her hair probably would have been enough. He'd kissed her because he hadn't been able to stop himself, and that just wouldn't fly. The woman was taken.

Except she seemed like the most inexperienced of lambs. What kind of a man was she engaged to? One who didn't even realize she was a woman, and that women needed to be caressed and desired?

Hot anger shot through Spencer. The paper wrinkled in his hands. He didn't know who he was more upset with, Kate's fiancé or himself.

And now she was hiding in her room. He knew that as sure as he knew his own name. And he had a very good feeling that his grandmother knew the same thing, even though she wouldn't know the reason why.

Well, damn, but he had chased her into a corner. It was up to him to coax her out. He had never frightened a woman in his life, and he wasn't about to start now. If she wanted a man who never touched her, so be it. He could at least let her know that he wouldn't assault her again. He only hoped that she'd believe him. He'd already kissed her twice in as many days.

Spencer set the paper aside.

His grandmother was smiling at him. "Well, are you going to go after her or aren't you?"

He smiled and shook his head. "Are all grandmothers as pushy as you?"

"If they're smart and their grandsons are blockheads who refuse to give them great-grandchildren, then yes, they probably are.''

"I'm a blockhead?''

She shrugged. ''You're down here and the woman you're clearly besotted with is upstairs. You figure it out.''

She had a point. A man who was deeply in love wouldn't just sit downstairs nonchalantly studying the day's news while the woman of his heart hid from him. He was supposed to be acting as if he cared about Kate, so why wasn't he with her?

Because this was all an act, of course. And because she was engaged. And also because he was probably the last person she wanted to see right now.

"Are you sure you didn't have a fight?''

Spencer looked down his nose at his grandmother. ''Don't push it, Grandmother.''

She wrinkled her nose. ''All right, that was over the line. I'll just go see what Connor and Bridget and Angela are up to, all right?''

"That's an excellent idea. And Grandmother?''

"Yes?''

"I think it would be best if the entire family is not waiting for us when Kate and I come downstairs. I wouldn't want her to feel uncomfortable.''

"Of course, dear. How long have you known Kate, anyway? You never said, and I don't recall you mentioning her name before.''

Spencer smiled. ''Not long, Grandmother.''

But he knew that time didn't really matter. His grandmother believed in love at first sight, and he could tell from her secret smile that she was thoroughly enjoying this whole scenario. Well, that was what he'd wanted when he'd planned this charade, wasn't it? Unfortunately, he hadn't figured Kate or Kate's feelings into the equation. That had been a mistake.

He schooled himself not to take the steps two at a time. He forced himself to knock on her door softly.

The door opened. Kate stood there in a pair of white shorts and a lilac T-shirt, barefoot, a baby in her arms. She could have been a stunning ad for fresh-faced beauty and absolute innocence.

"Spencer, I—"

He looked down at her bare feet. "You don't look as if you were planning on coming downstairs anytime soon. Aren't you hungry?"

He was. Exceptionally hungry, but only for forbidden fruit. For the taste of Kate's mouth. It was an indulgence he was going to have to deny himself.

Still, he was obviously doing a terrible job of hiding his desires. A light blush turned Kate's cheeks an endearing rose. "I would have come down eventually, but your grandmother said that you were a late sleeper, and I...well, I'm a Mom. I didn't want to neglect Toby."

Spencer turned to the blue-eyed, smiling cherub. "He looks pretty upset."

"He hides it well," Kate said, but she smiled and chuckled. "And all right, yes, maybe I was the one feeling neglected. He seemed to switch his allegiance to your grandmother with no problem. I guess I'm used to being his only caretaker."

"And you missed him."

She lifted one shoulder, clearly embarrassed to be caught in a vulnerable moment. "I missed him," she agreed.

"I should have known and planned activities that included your son."

"You didn't plan on having a child here when you decided to hire someone." She shifted Toby to her other hip.

"Doesn't matter. I spend my life adapting services to suit people's needs. And you have needs."

His voice dipped low on the last words and her blush deepened. Would an experienced woman do that? he wondered, realizing that none of the women he knew blushed. But it really didn't matter, did it? What he'd said was only the truth. She and her son were a package deal, and a child's needs came first in his world.

"There's a small beach at the end of the property. I'll bet we could manage to round up a few sand toys. Would you like that, big guy?" he asked, and he smiled at the child and held out his hands so that Toby would have the choice of going or staying.

Toby squealed and bucked in his mother's arms. He reached out his arms.

"Fickle little thing," Kate whispered as she kissed her son's dark curls and placed him in Spencer's arms.

"Big," Toby crowed, clapping his hands.

Spencer cocked his head and looked toward Kate.

"He's not used to men," she said. "I guess your arms ride a bit higher than mine."

"Ah, I'm a novelty, then. Novelty is good." He eyed Kate, who squirmed.

"So, I'm a novelty?" she asked.

"I've never dated a mother before."

"We're not dating," she reminded him as she grabbed a diaper bag and hunted for her shoes.

"Well then, I've never *pretended* to date a mother before."

She smiled at him from her upside-down position beneath the bed, dragging out a sandal. Spencer tried not to notice the curves that her position exposed.

"Have you pretended to date many women before?"

"Dozens."

"Liar. Your grandmother is much too curious about who I am and why I'm here for me to believe that."

"Well, I've definitely never dated an engaged woman before."

And her movements stilled. She quietly found the missing sandals and slipped them on.

"Kate?"

She looked up at him holding her son. She took a deep breath. "Is the beach close by or do we need to drive?"

"It's close," he said, but he wasn't really thinking about the location of the beach. He was thinking about the scared expression in Kate's eyes.

And once again Spencer was faced with the possibility that something wasn't right. No doubt he should never have hired a woman he had a history with, even if it was a minor history. Their shared past made him too curious and had him caring about things he shouldn't even be considering.

He'd brought her here to make his grandmother come alive with questions and possibilities, and now *he* was the one filled with a hundred questions. And some of those questions had to do with what it would be like to make love with Kate. Which meant only one thing. He ought to forget this whole scenario and free her from her obligations to him. Immediately.

"Let's go," he said. "Ready to hit the beach, big guy?" he asked the child in his arms.

"Go," Toby said, and when he looked up, something happened. Even though Toby was not actually Kate's son, he was of the same gene pool, and there was something of the wonder she'd once had that shone through the boy's eyes. Spencer couldn't help but question what had happened to that valiant little girl and why the grown woman no longer believed in dreams and didn't like talking about her engagement.

"Go?" Toby asked again, patting Spencer on the cheek.

"You bet," Spencer forced himself to shake away his troublesome thoughts. "Let's just stop and see if we can't find some toys and then we'll be off."

Spencer waited for Kate to move ahead of him and then he carried Toby down the stairs and out to the storage shed. He handed Kate the pail and shovel that Benton, the gardener, scoured up for him. Then he took Kate by the hand.

"Looks like we're set. To the sand castle." He winked at Kate.

"Lead on," she agreed with a small smile, but she still looked a bit concerned.

"Don't worry, I'm not going to kiss you again once I get you away from the house, Kate."

"I wasn't worried about that." She lifted her chin bravely, her words an obvious lie.

"You don't need to apologize. You don't even need to explain why you still kiss like an untutored schoolgirl," he said softly.

Fire flashed in her eyes. Finally. A trace of the Kate he'd once known.

"I was never an untutored schoolgirl."

Which was a terrible lie, but he liked the fact that there was still a bit of bravado in her. As children, he had sometimes tried to get his way by claiming male superiority. Kate had never let him get away with such tripe. She'd planted those little fists on her hips and declared that she was every bit as deserving as he was of being the leader in their games. She was going to be just as grand a winner in life as he was.

"Some people just aren't as physical as others," she continued when he hadn't answered.

He glanced down into her deep green eyes. "Ah, you're not physical? You don't like kissing?"

That lovely blush charged up her neck. She had appeared untutored but not indifferent to him.

"There's more to life than kissing, Spencer."

He chuckled then.

"Are you laughing at me?"

"I'm delighted by you. You are an amazing woman. You never give an inch, do you?"

And the air seemed to seep out of her. "I let you talk me into this horrible situation."

"I know. I'm sorry." He gently squeezed her hand. "But this is the third day. Only four more after today is done. Can you hold out?"

She gave a great sigh and looked down at their hands joined together, his large one enfolding her much smaller one. "I like your grandmother. She's very sweet and very smart, and I think she's enjoying herself. She likes Toby and she likes wondering what's going on between you and me. How can I regret anything that gives such a woman pleasure?

And besides, Toby likes her, too. He's having a good time. He can laugh and cry and babble to his heart's content. He can run without me having to warn him that the landlord likes us to be quiet. And the money you donated to Safe House will go a long way. I would be a fool to regret any of that.''

"But you do regret, don't you?"

They had arrived at the small gate that led to the beach and Spencer let Toby slide down from his arms. He and Kate watched as the little boy ran through the gate, plopped down in the sand and proceeded to sift the fine stuff through his tiny fingers.

"My mother and sister were both irrational dreamers. They loved playacting, they *lived* playacting, but the trouble was that they didn't seem to be able to separate their dreams, their acting from reality. We were a strange family, never able to get ahead, never able to even eat half the time and certainly never able to settle down and face the truths of life and get by the way other people did. We were always chasing things that weren't real. Disappointment was a regular guest in our house, but that didn't seem to change things. I swore I would never be that way. I worked my way through school, I vowed to live my life on solid ground, so no, I can't feel comfortable in a pretend situation like this. I'm afraid I'm not very good at acting.''

The wistful sound of her voice caught Spencer like a fist in the chest. He looked down at the deeply troubled expression in her green eyes.

"Then you don't need to act," he said softly, brushing back a few windblown wisps of her hair that had snagged on her lips. "We'll be just what we are, a man and woman who've come together to give your little guy a few days of freedom and to lend a few smiles to a woman on the verge of her birthday. We don't have to be more than that, Kate. My grandmother is happy simply because you're here, and I doubt if anything can spoil that now. So we can coast from here on out. We don't have to kiss.''

She blinked at that. She swallowed hard. She blushed. He loved it. He wondered at it.

"Tell me about him, Kate. Tell me all about this man you're going to marry.''

Chapter Six

Kate felt as if the sun had disappeared even though it was still shining brightly.

"Fitz, you mean?"

"Yes."

"What do you want to know? *Why* do you want to know?"

He blinked. "You'd be within your rights to tell me that I have no business asking, you know."

She knew, but she couldn't tell him that her engagement was none of his business. She couldn't say why. Instead, she just gazed up into Spencer's deep blue eyes and waited.

"You told me that you wouldn't want to love, so I'm assuming that it's not a love match."

"No."

He glanced at Toby and smiled as the little boy threw a handful of sand in the air and then sputtered when it rained down on him. Spencer kneeled and brushed the baby clean.

"Sand," Toby said, gazing up with adoring eyes. Kate couldn't help wondering if she looked that adoring when she looked at Spencer. The possibility made her stomach flutter and churn. Panic began to swirl through her.

"What does your fiancé, Fitz, do? Why did he let you come with me without any objections?" He looked over the baby's head and his gaze piniored her where he stood.

It seemed to Kate that the unspoken question shimmered between them. *Why don't you know more about kissing when you're on the verge of getting married?*

"What's he like?" Spencer said. "Should I call and allay any concerns he has about your being here? Should I apologize to you and him for anything I've done in the past few days?"

Please don't offer to apologize to anyone, Kate thought. That will only make it worse.

Where to begin? What to tell him? She thought of all the things she'd told her boss in the past few months and realized that she'd gotten very good at making up stories. Tales of romantic dinners for two, long walks in the rain, what it would be like to be married to a man who traveled as much as her Fitz did. She opened her mouth to begin another story.

And then she looked back at Spencer. Concern burned in his blue eyes.

Kate sighed. She sank to the sand beside Spencer and Toby.

"I don't know what to say, but...there's a reason I kiss the way I do. I haven't done much of it. My fiancé isn't real," she said softly. "He's an illusion, a convenience."

She expected him to be shocked, to yell, to frown at least. Instead, he only gave her a sad smile. "I didn't mean that comment about your kissing as an insult, you know. You kiss delightfully, Kate."

She blushed.

"And I probably shouldn't have said that," he added. "So you made your fiancé up?"

"Yes."

"Why?"

She took her child up on her lap and cuddled him close. When he squirmed to get back near the sand and she realized that *she* was the one in need of comfort, she let him go.

"I've never wanted to get romantically involved. Those kinds of dreams nearly destroyed my mother time and time again. My sister would go without food or clothing or proper shelter if she thought she was in love. She'd let a man rule her mind and her life and sometimes mistreat her. She'd have his baby out of wedlock and practically kill herself to give him everything he needed while she went without the basic necessities of life. I don't think she even realized she was doing those things. I'm not even sure the man always demanded she be that way. She was just enslaved by her own emotions. My mother was, too.

"I don't intend to live that way, and I don't want to fall in love. But sometimes people—men—don't understand. My boss is like that. He's a bit of a romantic himself. He thinks he's in love with me, and he won't take no for an answer. He never seems to give up, so…" She held out her hands.

"You gave him a reason to give up."

She nodded and looked away. "I know it sounds immature."

"I don't know about that. It must be difficult to work for someone and be dependent on them when they want more out of a relationship than you do and when they won't see reason. I'm sure you used reason at the beginning."

Kate blinked. "I most certainly did. I explained my position. I assured him that we would not suit. I was patient and understanding, but firm. I turned him down every time he asked me to dinner. I explained that I did not date my employers." She looked meaningfully at Spencer.

He grinned and held up his hands defensively. "I always listen when a woman says no."

She wondered if that had ever happened. She was tempted to ask, but she managed to contain her curiosity. Barely.

"He's not a bad man, I don't think. If he were, I'd look for another job elsewhere, even though I love my work and even though it would be inconvenient to leave when I have a child to care for, but he's just so…"

"Unconvinced."

"Exactly." She couldn't keep the confusion from her voice.

Spencer chuckled and she raised her chin and faced him.

"You think it's funny?"

"Not at all. I'm sorry you have to put up with such an uncomfortable situation. I have no tolerance for any man who would try to push himself on an unwilling woman, and I'd gladly deck him if you asked me to, but I understand why your boss isn't buying into your story, Kate."

"Because he's never seen Fitz or met him?" She

wondered how long she'd been in the habit of almost believing the existence of the fictional "Fitz" herself. She certainly talked about him as if he were real.

"Because you don't seem like a woman who's getting married, Kate. I've known plenty of engaged women, I've admired more than a few, and there's an air of power, of excitement, an energy that almost causes the air around them to shimmer. But there's more to it than that. You're just too innocent, Kate."

She frowned. "The untutored schoolgirl."

"I'm sorry I put it that way."

A sigh escaped her lips. "You were only being honest. At any rate, I'm sorry I deceived you. I'm certainly not placing you in the same category as my boss. It wasn't that I thought I needed protection from you."

"Maybe you're wrong about that. I'm definitely attracted to you. I've kissed you twice."

"You had good reasons."

He lifted one corner of his lips in a wry smile. "Thank you for being so generous, but I'm not going to lie, Kate. I liked kissing you too much, and while I'll try my best not to take advantage of our situation, I'm only human, and this situation is—"

"Impossible," she said, repeating her earlier conviction.

He shrugged. "It's a bit of a minefield. You're very tempting, Kate. I'll do my best to be a gentleman. Thank you for telling me the truth. I think."

"You'd rather not have known?"

He shook his head. "I didn't say that, but your fiancé did provide me with a convenient barrier, even if I thought the man was a bit slow."

She blinked in confusion, and his answering laughter was low and deep and delicious.

"The man obviously didn't take you into his arms nearly enough," he whispered, "or you wouldn't have been so flustered by a man's touch."

"Maybe you're just a man who flusters me," she said, and that was the truth. She had the feeling that she could have been kissed a thousand times and Spencer's kisses would still have left her breathless. "Maybe we should continue to pretend that Fitz exists?"

He smiled. "We could try. What did you say he looked like? Short, balding, a bit puffy about the eyes?"

She grinned at him. "Tall, blond, very Nordic-looking. Lots of muscles."

"Hmm, I'll have to be careful then that I don't offend him, won't I?"

"Absolutely."

They both laughed. Toby threw another handful of sand in the air and laughed, too.

"I wish Ruth could see him now," Kate said.

"I'm sure if she could—if she can—then she's happy that you're the one caring for him."

"I hope so. I'm not sure if she'd approve of my methods. Not enough make-believe."

"Then maybe we could have some make-believe right now."

Kate looked at him in alarm.

He shook his head. "I'm not talking about your situation with me and my grandmother. Looks like we've got a perfectly good stretch of sand and we've got a source of water," he said, indicating the lake. "And over here we have a little boy, a bucket and a shovel, as well as numerous sticks, which are always good for digging. I used to be pretty adept at making sand castles. Why don't we give it a try?''

His expression dared her to say yes, and Kate's breath caught. "I don't know," she said. "I never really made sand castles. I was too busy being the practical Ryerson."

Spencer raised one eyebrow. "I don't think you'll lose your title as 'the practical Ryerson' if you make just one sand castle. If you want it to remain a secret, I'll never tell, and I'm pretty sure Toby won't mind, will you, big guy?''

Toby looked up at Spencer with big, round eyes. "Guy," he said.

Spencer chuckled and knelt beside him. "That's us—guys. And your mom here is a pretty lady."

Toby smiled. "Lady," he agreed.

"That's right. Let's see if we can't get her to help us build a castle, okay?''

"'Kay," Toby said.

"See, he's all for the idea."

She couldn't help laughing. "He doesn't have a clue what you mean."

"But he's willing to go along."

Kate had a feeling that a lot of people were willing to go along with whatever Spencer suggested. A man shouldn't be allowed to have such an engaging smile. But half an hour later she was glad she had fallen in with the project. Spencer was an expert castle builder, but he didn't let his expertise get in the way of Toby's fun. He carried water for Toby, encouraged him to pat the wet sand to his heart's content even though more patting than building got done, and he viewed Toby's efforts with an intentionally blind eye.

"Whoa, that's one great tower," he said, helping Toby unearth his wobbly, misshapen creation from the bucket. "Now let's add a flag to the top, shall we?"

"Flag."

"Yeah, what can we use? How about a nice fat leaf?" And he scooped up an elm leaf that had blown from a nearby tree. He poked two holes in the leaf and impaled it on a twig. "Put it in our tower," Spencer suggested, showing Toby what to do.

With chubby fingers and an overabundance of enthusiasm Toby tried to shove the twig into the wet tower, but his little hand hit the edge and the tower began to crumble.

Toby's lower lip trembled.

Kate started to reach for him.

"Hey, that's okay, Toby," Spencer said before she could get to Toby. "Happens to the best castle builders. Now here's what we do," and he took Toby onto his lap. Together they removed the twig, laid it aside, then scooped the wet sand back into the pail, little hands patting it down next to Spencer's big hands. Then Spencer helped Toby place his palms on either side of the plastic bucket and together they tipped it upside down and re-formed the tower.

"Now let's just put our flag back in," Spencer said softly.

Toby looked straight up, tilting his chin high as he tried to see Spencer's face. He didn't reach for the flag.

"Want help?" Spencer asked.

Toby didn't answer, but he kept his eyes on Spencer.

"Together then," Spencer said, and he took Toby's

tiny hands in his own. Together they carefully picked up the spindly leaf flag.

"Now hold your breath, buddy," Spencer whispered as he guided Toby and helped him apply enough pressure to push the flag into the sand without disturbing the tower. When the flag was carefully seated, he let out his breath.

"That is one great castle, Toby," he said. "Looks good."

"Good," Toby agreed, latching on to the familiar word.

"Looks very good," Spencer said, and he smiled at Kate.

She couldn't help it. She smiled back. "Thank you," she said. "You should have children."

He shrugged. "Maybe someday I will."

"I thought that wasn't in the plans."

"No." He shook his head and dusted off Toby's wet, sandy hands. "I said that love wasn't in my plans. Someday I'll get married. I'd like to have children, and I intend to love them. It's only romantic love that I'm opposed to. I definitely don't want—in fact, I refuse to have—anything so irrational or threatening in my life."

"Wise man," she agreed, but there was a strange sad shifting feeling just beneath her heart. Women would naturally have romantic thoughts about a man like Spencer. Women who would get caught up in hopeless dreams the way her sister and mother had. No doubt he would break many hearts even if he didn't intend to. And the woman he would eventually marry?

Kate didn't want to think about that, but she did. Whoever and wherever the woman was, Kate felt sorry for her. She would probably spend her life guarding her heart against falling in love with Spencer. Still, he was a natural-born father. She hoped he found someone who would appreciate that.

"We'd better get back home," Spencer said, lifting Toby and dusting him off. He placed Toby into Kate's waiting arms and picked up the diaper bag and toys.

"Will your grandmother be worried?"

Spencer chuckled. "No, I know these grounds intimately. If we don't show up soon, she might even be encouraged. Maybe she'll think that I've eloped with you."

Kate almost gasped. "She wouldn't think that."

Spencer reached out with his free hand and traced a gentle line along Kate's cheek. "I'm teasing, Kate."

She blinked. Of course, she should have known that. But she was beginning to think that where Spencer was concerned, she didn't have a clue what she was doing. His slightest touch jumbled her thought processes.

"I only meant that we should get back so that you and Toby could have lunch," he explained.

"All right." But she wished they didn't have to go back to the house. For the short time they had been here, she had felt free to just enjoy her son and to savor the moment.

But once she returned to the house, she would be Spencer's woman again, and anything could happen.

Spencer walked along beside Kate, occasionally turning to look at her. Every time he turned, the solemn blue-eyed baby was gazing at him worshipfully. Spencer ruffled the little boy's silky dark curls.

There was something very warm and right about

this picture, a man, a woman and a child coming home from a day spent playing in the sand.

There was also something very wrong with this picture and the something wrong was his own intense reaction to Kate.

She wasn't engaged. There was no man to stand in his way if he wanted to kiss her, to hold her. The man that had kept him from her didn't even exist. The thought ran through his head, and his chest felt tight. Exultation flooded his soul. Alarm bells sounded. Long, loud, growing louder and more frantic every second. Tension crept into his consciousness, dark and angry and merciless.

There was no barrier here at all, and dammit, he wanted barriers. High ones. Impenetrable ones, covered in barbed wire with huge Keep Out, No Trespassing signs. Or maybe what he really wanted—what he needed above all—was simply a woman who didn't make him ache to move closer.

Kate made him want to move so close that he was actually inside her skin. He didn't like that at all, especially after a lifetime spent avoiding such feelings. He would do almost anything—including ignoring his own most basic needs—to obliterate such emotions from his world.

So he was going to have to learn to curb his reactions to Kate. He intended to start learning how to do that immediately. No doubt he could come up with some sort of mental game to keep him from thinking about the taste of her lips or how her body had felt pressed against his own. The mind was very powerful.

All he had to do was concentrate.

But as he neared the back entrance of the house after dropping off the pail and shovel in the storage shed, his attention was distracted by the sound of voices coming from the tiered patio at the back of the house.

"I'm not trying to cause trouble. I just don't want to upset your grandmother by leaving so soon. She invited me here." Angela said.

"You know why she invited you here," Connor answered. "She invited you here for Spencer, but Spencer's clearly taken."

"Connor, you're such a…a man." The sound of Angela's low laughter drifted by, and Spencer glanced at Kate, who was looking right back at him. "You don't really think Spencer's taken, do you? At least not for good?"

"What's that supposed to mean?" Connor was clearly not amused.

"Connor, open your eyes," Angela said.

"Believe me, Angela, my eyes are always open where women are concerned. So what are you implying? Are you trying to insult Spencer and Kate?"

She laughed. "On the contrary, I like them both immensely. I simply mean that their situation isn't as cut-and-dried as it seems at first glance."

"Things seldom are. What are you really doing here, Angela?" His voice softened slightly. "The last time I saw you, you were breaking my best friend's heart."

His comment was followed by silence. "Well, as you say, things are seldom as clear as they seem. And I'm here because I was invited. For your brother. And Bridget is here for you," she said firmly.

Spencer leaned toward Kate and cupped his hand close by her ear. "Maybe we should take a detour around the side."

But Kate had a look of defiance in her eye and a definite stubborn tilt to her chin. "Maybe we should put in an appearance, just for appearance's sake."

"I told you that you didn't have to pretend anymore."

"I know, but that's what you hired me to do. I always do my job, Spencer."

For some reason, some small part of him felt a bit disgruntled at being considered a job even though that was exactly what he was, but another part of him couldn't help admiring the purposeful way Kate turned toward the patio. She stopped near the edge, kissed her child and gave him to Spencer, waiting until he had him resting safely on his left hip. Then she linked her right arm with Spencer's and pressed herself up against his body.

He almost thought he heard her take a breath and whisper, "Here goes," but he couldn't be sure about that.

"Kate," he whispered, bending near her ear so that anyone out of hearing range would think that he was nuzzling her.

"Yes?" Her voice could barely be heard, it was so soft.

"You really, really don't have to do this. My grandmother seems happy enough as things are."

"But if people continue whispering about us behind her back, she's bound to hear sooner or later. Even a hint of discord might be troublesome to her. She might be hurt or worried and she shouldn't be that, not with her birthday coming up. I like her. Let's at least give her a few days of happiness. I'm not a big believer in dreams, but I've seen how painful it can be to give one up. Your grandmother shouldn't have her dreams trampled just before her special day.''

He stared down at her and was surprised at the defiant look in her eyes. He was also touched by this gesture of hers. He'd offered her the easy way out, and she wasn't going to take it even though pretending to be a man's lover made her extremely uncomfortable. He suddenly wanted to make things easy for her, but he couldn't deny the truth of her words. His grandmother had had a difficult time these past few years. She'd lost her husband, she'd lost her son, she'd lost many of her friends, but right now she was enjoying herself. Was it so wrong to give her a few more days of fun?

"All right, and thank you, but if we're going to go back to pretending, we're not resurrecting Fitz, too, are we?" he asked with a teasing smile.

Kate looked up at him with wide eyes, and carefully crossed her heart. "Fitz is out of town," she promised with an impish smile.

"Keep him there," he whispered.

And he wondered why he suddenly cared about an imaginary lover, the man Kate had dreamed up as the perfect mate.

Of course, he didn't care. He was just fascinated by Kate and what made a woman like her tick. Like the fact that she cared about and would sacrifice herself to help down-on-their-luck children. She'd spent her childhood being the practical Ryerson, helping to hold her family together, and she wanted to make things right for an old woman on her birthday. A woman like that deserved admiration and all the support a man could give her.

"Spencer," Connor said, smiling at the three of them. "We were just talking about you."

Spencer smiled at the mischievous twinkle in his brother's eyes. "Good things, I hope."

"Of course good things. Ah, I see Kate is here, too. You must be a very special lady. I was just wondering about you. How did the two of you end up together? My brother has never brought a woman to a family gathering before."

Spencer frowned at Connor. There was a decided air of danger about his younger brother today. He was in a bad mood, and now he was aiming his attention at Kate.

"That's enough, Connor. Leave her alone," he warned.

But he hadn't counted on Kate. The woman couldn't be trusted to stay in the background just because he was willing to shield her. An image of that little girl with her hands on her hips demanding that he marry her someday rose before him.

"Don't worry, I'm fine, Spencer," she said, placing her fingers on his sleeve. "Of course your brother has questions, and I don't mind answering them."

But even through the cotton of his white shirt, he could feel her fingers trembling. Spencer folded his hand over hers, trying to warm and reassure her.

"If you have anything to ask, Connor, ask me," he suggested. "Let's leave Kate out of this."

Chapter Seven

Kate looked across the patio. Connor and Angela were studying her with interest. She realized that she was clutching Spencer's arm rather hard and started to free herself, but he applied gentle pressure and held her there. An almost visible tension flowed from him. Because his brother had questioned her, and he was going to protect her?

Oh no, she couldn't afford to start depending on a man to fight her battles for her. Kate tugged her hand free. She stepped away from Spencer, although she continued to gaze up at him with what she hoped the room would read as adoration.

Spencer's attention was fully on her, his eyes staring directly into her own, and her heart begin to trip wildly.

She steeled her mind to focus on her performance. "So Spencer doesn't usually bring women to visit at family gatherings? I suppose I should be flattered then," she said, smiling at Spencer.

"As I said, you're the first," Connor agreed. "There must be something very special or different about you."

"Actually, Spencer and I go way back," she said, and this time she didn't have to inject any emotion in her voice. A memory of Spencer kneeling to brush off her knee when she'd once fallen and scraped herself played through her mind, and her voice automatically softened. She looked at him and wondered how much he remembered of those days.

"Way back," he whispered in a voice that sounded like a caress. He stepped closer, leaning to place his lips so near her ear that the warmth of his breath was like a caress. "Weren't we once even engaged?" he whispered.

Embarrassing warmth stole up Kate's body. She quickly looked away and noticed that Angela was wearing a gentle, knowing smile. The expression in Connor's eyes could only be described as intense concern. Kate realized that Connor might well have gone through many of the same painful experiences with his father that Spencer had. For some crazy reason she wanted to tell him not to worry. She couldn't possibly damage his brother in any way. Instead, she simply smiled at him.

"I feel blessed to have this time with your family," she said, and she realized that she was telling the truth. Her mother had left her employ at Spencer's summer home suddenly, called away by an overpowering whim, something that had seemed terribly important and all-consuming at the time no doubt, Kate seemed to remember. She hadn't even gotten to say goodbye to Spencer. She'd never even met Connor. Spencer had told her that his little brother was away at camp that year. It had been an oddly compelling summer of magic and dreams, and while she'd given up the dreams voluntarily, the abrupt ending to one of her last bits of childhood had left her with a feeling of something not quite finished. She'd thought of Spencer now and then and wished she could put away those childhood memories completely. Now at last, here in the heart of his family, she hoped she could do that. Finish things completely and tuck her girlish memories away forever.

"What do you want to know about me, Connor?" she asked.

Spencer moved even closer to her, a shield, Kate suspected. She glanced up and saw that Spencer's gaze, fixed on his brother, had turned cool. "Kate, you don't have to answer questions that make you uncomfortable," Spencer said. "My brother knows I have boundaries. He's in grave danger of crossing them right now."

But she shook her head. "He's your family, Spencer. He gets to be concerned."

She kept her eyes on Connor as she spoke, but as she finished speaking, Connor smiled and shook his head. He glanced toward his brother. "Spencer's right. I'm in a worse mood than usual today and I've stepped over the line. A bad habit we Fairfields have. We're all a bit overprotective, you know."

She knew. Hadn't Spencer hired her to protect his grandmother? Wasn't his grandmother trying to secure his happiness and Connor's? And wouldn't she do the same thing for Toby? Hadn't she always been that way with Ruth and her mother?

"You don't have to apologize to me. I understand completely."

"Somehow I believe you," Connor said, but he looked beyond her as a noise was heard at the door.

"Here you all are," Loretta Fairfield said, sweeping onto the patio with Bridget and a quartet of men and women. "We have more guests. Distant cousins. The party is beginning in earnest, my dears. Come here and meet everyone. Connor, you haven't spoken to Bridget all day."

Connor gave Kate, Angela and Spencer a brittle smile and went to do his duty.

And Kate found Spencer at her back. He bent toward her. "I hope you're going to be just as honored to meet my family when all my distant relatives begin descending on us," he whispered. "Connor was right when he said that I never bring anyone. You'll be the star attraction. And Kate?"

"Yes?" she answered breathlessly as his deep voice rumbled through her body.

"Thank you for these past few minutes. You're a very magnificent lady." And he dropped the lightest of kisses on the top of her head. A completely innocent touch, but she breathed in deeply, her body turned warm, then cold, then warmer still.

"I—you're welcome. Anytime."

He chuckled. "Don't make any rash promises you'll regret."

Oh, but in many ways she'd already done that. Every time Spencer touched her, she regretted any number of things. Like the fact that she would never truly be free to touch back without fear of dire consequences.

"Should we go meet everyone?" she suggested, trying to steer her thoughts down safer paths.

"Very briefly. You still haven't been fed, and

Toby's getting drowsy.'' He nodded toward the child falling asleep in the crook of his arm. ''There are bounds beyond which I cannot go, Kate, and I won't have you giving up nourishment or rest for me.''

Spencer was as good as his word. After introducing her to the cousins, he informed his grandmother that he was taking Kate and Toby off to feed them. Within thirty minutes, Kate had eaten, and Spencer had escorted her to her room, helped her put Toby to bed and was leaving. ''I know you're not a child like Toby, but you might consider taking a nap, too,'' he suggested. ''I suspect that the evening is going to be a bit trying for you. More relatives and neighbors arriving for a small dinner party. Will you be all right? We don't have to go.''

She chuckled. ''What excuse could we make?''

He grinned. ''I could tell my grandmother that we had a mad longing to be alone. We could watch the sun set from the dock. She'd be delighted, and you could get away from the crowds.''

And spend time alone with Spencer at sunset? There was so much more danger there than a roomful of curious relatives could provide.

She took a deep breath. ''I choose the party,'' she said, trying to ignore her own sense of loss. A sunset with Spencer sounded heavenly.

Which was why she'd turned it down. All she had to do was think of her sister tripping off and forgetting all reason and duty every time something tempting came along, and Kate knew she would cut off a body part before she'd ever follow the family tradition of falling hopelessly in love with an elusive dream.

''You're sure?''

She sighed. "The party," she said more firmly.

"The party it is then, Kate," Spencer said, chuckling.

She opened her eyes and frowned at him. "Are you laughing at me again, Spencer?"

"Never, sweet Kate. But I was just thinking that another man might be offended. You've chosen an evening with Uncle Horace and Aunt Betty over an interlude in the dark with me. You're very bad for my ego, you know."

She shook her head. "I have the feeling that you've had far too many women who were good for your ego, Spencer."

"Ah, but they weren't you, were they?" And he kissed her lightly and left her there.

She knew exactly what he meant. Though she tried to take a nap, she ended up tossing and turning. She had been kissed before, but never the way Spencer kissed her. Kate was beginning to understand her sister Ruth's favorite expression, "But I *need* to do this," usually voiced just before she had done something incredibly stupid with a man. Something that left her smiling, but which held no future.

"Oh no, that's not me," Kate told herself.

Tonight she would spend her time with Spencer's relatives and keep her distance from the man. Because if she allowed herself to get close to him, she just might "pull a Ruth" and beg him to take her out on the dock to watch the sunset.

And once she was alone with Spencer in the dark, who knew what she might want to do?

Spencer perused the crowded room and he wondered if it was too soon to rescue Kate. The evening was every bit as trying as he had thought it would be. She was besieged by well-meaning relatives asking her everything from questions about her family to ones about her future plans.

Uncle Horace came right out and asked her if she was going to marry his nephew.

"Don't badger her, Horace," Spencer said. "She's my guest."

"I'm just asking."

"Then don't."

"Does that mean the answer's no?"

"It means I don't want Kate being pressured by my family."

"But we like her. There's no harm in liking her, is there?"

Spencer almost couldn't hold back a sigh at that point, but Kate tugged on his sleeve. She looked up at Horace. "There's definitely no harm in liking another person. I'm not offended in the least, and if Spencer and I decide to get married, we'll let everyone know," she said sweetly.

Horace gave her a satisfied smile and toddled away, looking for a glass of wine.

Spencer slipped an arm around her waist and walked with her. "You're an angel. Have I told you that?"

Her laughter was low and sweet and incredulous. "I don't think I've sprouted wings yet, no."

"That's just because they're pinned to your back. You can't see them like the rest of us can. Or your halo, either." He brushed one finger over a silky strand of her hair. "It's attached up here somewhere. I'm sorry about all that, by the way. Uncle Horace isn't normally so bad. He's just—"

"I know. He's an overprotective Fairfield."

Spencer chuckled. "I suppose that's true, but I was going to say that he's not able to handle wine all that well."

"Me, neither. Don't let me drink any more."

He looked down at her empty glass and grinned. "Some men would view that as an opportunity."

"Maybe, but not you. You're not that kind of man. Spencer Fairfield looks after the weak and the elderly, and I'm pretty sure you look after mildly tipsy women, too. Isn't that true?"

He shrugged. "I have my weaknesses, yes."

"Or strengths. Poor Bridget."

Spencer looked up at the frail redhead who was dancing with Connor and obviously not enjoying herself. "I wonder that she's still here."

"I don't know, but I think she's unhappy. Maybe she thought your brother would make her happy, but it's not going to happen. She's disappointed and maybe even a bit afraid of him."

"Connor's angry about something. For some reason I don't understand, he's hurting. Ordinarily, he's a gentle man."

She smiled. "And you would protect him if you could. Well, in spite of his frowns, I believe he *is* a gentle man, but I think Bridget needs more than a gentle man. And she's upset because Connor's not what she expected. Your grandmother wouldn't have mentioned the scowls."

"I don't think Grandmother ever mentions our flaws. Maybe she doesn't even admit we have any. Everything we do is seen through love-filtered glasses. But Connor doesn't like it when she sets us up with dates. He was deeply affected by what happened to my father and grandmother, but in a different way. Because Connor actually bought into the family curse. He once thought he'd found his soul mate. She didn't agree, although she gladly took his gifts and all that he could offer...for a while. Now he's not sure what he believes. He's been a bit leery of women and their intentions since then. He's especially suspicious of the women who come here at my grandmother's behest, because he's certain that the family fortune figures strongly in their reasons for being here.''

''And does it?''

''Most times,'' he agreed. ''My grandmother doesn't see it, and I can't be sure of everyone, but yes, I think that perhaps Bridget was hoping for a nice shy, retiring rich man. Connor must be a disappointment since he's neither shy nor retiring. But as I said, he's not normally such a thundercloud.''

''He seems to be indifferent to Bridget, but Angela...that's different. She bothers him. A lot.''

''Because she was meant for me. Connor's always been angrier about me than about himself. I think he's afraid I'll succumb one day and end up like my father. And...how can I put this delicately? I've dated women who look like Angela before.''

He felt rather than heard Kate take a deep breath. ''Of course. I think I've seen some pictures. I—Spencer, you know I only agreed to this because I thought this was what you wanted, but if you would rather—''

''Shh, don't.'' He placed his fingertips lightly against her lips. ''Don't say it. I could have brought someone like Angela, but I chose you. I'm not even remotely attracted to Angela.''

Kate looked up at him, her green eyes dark as she studied him. "That's good."

"It is?"

"Yes, of course. I wouldn't want it to look as though I was standing between you and a woman you wanted."

He could have told her that there was only one woman he wanted right now, but that would be a mistake. He didn't even want to examine the implications of why he'd chosen her beyond the fact that he'd thought her to be an engaged woman, but he knew that there were other reasons.

"It's also good that you're not attracted to Angela, because I think that your brother *is*."

"Connor?"

"Do you have another brother?"

"He practically snaps her head off every time she speaks."

"Yes, he does, doesn't he? And even if he's attracted, he doesn't seem to like her very much. So many unhappy people," she said sadly.

"Are you unhappy? Have I made you unhappy by bringing you here, Kate?"

"No," she answered quickly. Too quickly, he thought, but before he had a chance to examine his reaction to Kate's predicament, his grandmother walked up beside them.

"I've just come from checking on your baby. He's such a wonder," she said to Kate. "Spencer, dear?"

"Yes, Grandmother."

"I wonder...it's getting close to sunset and it looks as if it's going to be a glorious one. Would you mind leading a group of people down to the dock? I would go, but you know how it is with me. Age is such a disappointment, dear Kate. It's a shame what getting old does to a person."

"You're not old. You're interesting," Kate said. She turned to Spencer. "Your grandmother told me that she once met Picasso. And that she went on safari in Africa."

Loretta chuckled. "Thank you for the compliment, dear, but unfortunately those things all happened years ago when my husband was still alive. I think I need to be here to make sure Horace stays upright. But if the two of you go, make sure there are enough blankets at the dock. It would be a great help. It gets a bit chilly once the sun starts going down."

Spencer turned to Kate. "Is that all right? If you're tired I can take you to your room and I'll tend to things."

"Oh, she's young, Spencer," his grandmother said. "And it's a beautiful spot for a sunset, Kate."

"Well then, I wouldn't miss it," Kate said, and she placed her hand in Spencer's as he led her away. Together they stopped and picked up blankets and a picnic basket loaded with thermoses of coffee from the kitchen.

"I guess we're not going to miss the sunset, after all," he said, referring to this afternoon's conversation.

"Well, it *has* been a while since I've stopped to watch the sun go down. Might be even longer before I get the chance again."

Together they strolled across the rolling grass headed toward the lake.

"What a lovely evening," Kate said, lifting her face to feel the warm night air.

"Perfect," he agreed. And the woman at his side

was even lovelier than the scenery. Her hand felt as if it had been created to match his own.

They walked on, and Spencer tried to ignore the urge to lift their joined hands and kiss Kate's fingertips. He did his best to concentrate on their destination. The dock was only a small distance from the house, but by the time they arrived, the sun was nearing the final drop stage.

Kate glanced back over her shoulder. She frowned. "That's funny. I thought the others were coming."

So had Spencer, but he had already noticed that no one was following. Or likely to now, given the time. "I have the feeling that my grandmother planned this. Maybe she thought that Uncle Horace was harassing you too much. Or maybe she was simply afraid that the relatives weren't showing well and were going to scare you away."

Kate smiled up at him and shook her head. "I suppose we should have known. It's our own fault. No one seemed the slightest bit eager to leave the party."

"Yes, Franklin was still serving wine and pâté."

They walked on a few more steps, stopping in the middle of the dock. The water gently rocked the large wooden structure, which contained several Adirondack chairs and a cushioned love seat of carved pine. The sky before them was a brilliant gold and red with deep purple at the edges. Beautiful, but soon darkness would cover everything.

He could kiss Kate.

It was as if the thought triggered an avalanche of desire in Spencer's soul. He ached to touch her, to cover her mouth with his own. He'd been pushing away the idea all day, but now there was near darkness, silence, stillness, the new knowledge that her lips and her kisses belonged to no other man.

Kate stood at his side, warm and scented of soap and lavender. He glanced down at the tendrils of her hair that brushed her cheeks and the pale skin above the neckline of her white dress. The need to hold her began to intensify.

Night was coming quickly now. If his lips roamed beyond Kate's lips to taste the hollow of her throat, if he slipped her free of her dress and trailed kisses over her shoulders and breasts, they would be alone in the shadows with only the water lapping against the dock for a companion.

"Kate," he whispered, and the dark beyond the glow of the setting sun seemed to deepen. The need to take her in his arms and make love to her surged more strongly.

She looked up at him, and he knew without question that his desire for her was written clearly in his eyes. She took a visible breath, her eyes widened, grew more languorous. She was not impervious to him, but aware of her as he was, he also noticed that her fingers were trembling. Clearly she felt desire but also a trace of panic.

He had brought her to this house, and except for her son, she was alone with no protector.

He could take advantage of that. He burned to take advantage of her. If he wanted her right now, he could have her. He could see that so clearly. He could also see that she was nothing like the women he was used to bedding. Tomorrow counted with her. If he took her, what would that make him?

What would it do to her?

"Go back to the house, Kate," he said suddenly,

his voice low and tight. "Now, before I start something we're both going to regret in the morning."

But she gazed up at him as if she was frozen in place, a bunny rabbit knowing it should run from the sight of a man with a gun but helpless to do so.

Her lips were parted slightly.

Spencer closed his eyes briefly, trying to gather more control, but when he opened them again, all he saw was a woman that he wanted very badly. "Kate, don't trust me. Please. I don't trust myself. If I touch you now, it won't be just a kiss this time. You know that."

For long seconds they stared at each other. Her scent filled his senses, her warmth drew him.

She leaned toward him slightly.

He reached for her. Deliberately. Slowly. He gave her one last chance.

"Kate?" He wanted her to run. He thought he'd surely die if she did.

She stared into his eyes, her own a deep green. She gave him no answer.

"So be it," he said. He stepped closer to her.

She swayed toward him. His body and hers were separated by only a breath.

He groaned. "Kate." His hand touched hers. Fire leaped within him, and he slid his hand up her arm. He stroked her shoulder, he slipped his fingers into her hair, cupping the back of her head as he lowered his mouth to hers.

When their lips met, flame flared inside him and he dragged her closer against him. He licked at the seam of her lips and she opened for him. She rested her hands on his chest, and he went half-crazy.

Lifting her in his arms, he brought her down his

body, his mouth lingering over the curve of her breast that swelled above her pale dress.

"Let me taste you, Kate," he whispered, and he bent to her. With one motion, he swept the straps of her dress aside, baring her breasts.

His breath nearly left him as he gazed at her, beautiful and half-naked as he took her into his arms. He touched his lips to the side of her neck, sending a shiver through her and a rush of dark passion through him. Only with great effort did he force himself to go slowly, to tend to her when he wanted to lower her to the ground and have her here. Now.

Her head fell back, and he swallowed hard. He kissed the peak of one pink-tipped breast.

She sighed, a sound that he'd heard from many women, but had never affected him so strongly. And never had he heard such a sigh from Kate.

And as if she'd just realized that same thing herself, as if that small sound had awakened her to reality, she squeezed her eyes closed. She went rigid and pulled away from him, desperately trying to repair the damage done to her hair and dress.

"No," she said, nearly choking on the word. "No, you were right before. This is…all wrong. So very wrong. I'm so extremely sorry. For a second I wanted to be like…maybe like Ruth was, but I just can't."

She fled into the night back toward the house. He watched her go. He stood there for long seconds as the ache inside him tightened and stabbed. He sank to the bare wood of the dock, his back against a guardrail at the edge. The sun slipped away completely, the darkness covered him, and finally, slowly, the tension in him, the weakness that had taken control of him began to release him from its clutches just the tiniest bit.

Spencer took deep breaths. He realized what he had almost done. Only the fact that he had released Kate the moment she had asked him to gave him any relief. Only the fact that she had had the sense to run gave him a sense of hope. "Good girl, Kate," he managed to say. If Kate hadn't gone, the consequences of this night would surely have been disastrous. Strength was so important to her. She would surely have seen her quick desire for him as a sign of unforgivable weakness reminiscent of her sister.

Besides, she'd had enough bumpy rides in her life. What she and her son needed was stability. A world where there were no complaining landlords or men who would take advantage of her situation. It was something to think about and remember.

He would do that, just as soon as his blood returned to a normal temperature and as soon as he could think clearly again. He had the terrible feeling, however, that he could never be near Kate without feeling hot and out of control. He could not touch her again. What if she hadn't stopped him and they had made a child together?

He wondered if she was thinking the same thing.

Chapter Eight

Kate could barely force herself to go downstairs the next morning. Had she really been so wanton in Spencer's arms the night before?

Ridiculous question. She had, even when he'd given her a chance to say no several times. She had wanted him to kiss her, to touch her. Deep inside she was still the girl who had wanted more than she could have.

Only she wasn't a girl anymore and she was very cognizant of the boundaries of her life. It was only a fluke that had brought her here with Spencer, and soon enough she would be gone. She'd be back to her landlord and boss, and she and Toby would be on their own.

"Don't make that mistake again," she warned herself as she marched down the hall, leaving a sleeping Toby in his crib.

"Sounds like you're beating up on yourself, but aren't we all allowed a few mistakes?" The voice came from the room she'd just passed, and Kate turned to find Angela leaning against the door frame. "Come inside. I could use some company," the beautiful blond woman said. "Want to talk about it?"

She would love to confide in another woman. She certainly didn't trust herself to listen to her own advice anymore, but she couldn't talk about Spencer to anyone. Most especially not to a stranger, and a guest in his grandmother's house.

"Thanks, but...I'm all right."

Angela smiled sadly. "Sure you are. Just like me. We all tend to go a bit nuts around the Fairfield men."

"You're disappointed that Spencer brought a friend with him." She'd thought her spirits couldn't go any lower, but she'd been wrong. The thought that Angela might begin pursuing him in earnest turned up her anxiety level another notch.

Angela shook her head and motioned Kate into her room. She shut the door. "Don't worry, I'm not interested in Spencer, and he's not interested in me."

Which was, of course, the polite thing to say. Still, Kate's attention was drawn away from the subject at hand immediately. On the bed lay a half-packed suitcase. "Are you leaving? Or maybe you just never unpacked?"

"Right the first time," Angela said with a shrug.

"But why? Not because of me? And don't bother telling me again that you're not interested in Spencer. You were invited here by his grandmother. If anyone should go, I should."

Angela shook her head, and her pretty blond hair brushed her shoulders. "I was brought here for Spencer, who doesn't want me, but that's not the whole reason I'm leaving."

"I don't understand."

"That's because you've never gotten mixed up with a Fairfield before."

"And you have." Kate struggled not to panic.

"Not Spencer."

"Connor."

"Yes. Sort of. I was engaged to his best friend three years ago. I broke off the engagement one week before the wedding. Connor's never forgiven me. I shouldn't have come, but I've known Loretta forever, I adore her, and…well, what can I say? I was hoping that he would have realized that I never meant to hurt Charles. I just couldn't marry him. I loved someone else. But then, none of that matters anymore. I'm off. My being here is just making everyone crazy."

"Angela, no."

The woman chuckled. "Angela, yes. I should have gone the minute I saw how things were."

Kate stared at the model-perfect woman and saw that there were tears in Angela's eyes. "Does Loretta know?"

Angela gave a watery laugh. "I certainly hope not. Especially since it was a complete mistake to come. The years away from Connor have only made things worse. He hates me more than ever now. If that is remotely possible."

Her voice dropped to a whisper on the last words. She turned her back and began shoving her clothes into the suitcase.

Kate came up behind her. "I'm so sorry, Angela. I wish I could help." But of course she couldn't. She knew better than anyone that love wasn't something a person could control. That was what made it so dangerous. The very thought sent fear spiraling through her. If she hadn't run last night, if she'd allowed herself to feel…

She hadn't. At least not too much, she hoped.

"Let me help you," she said again, forcing her thoughts away from her own problems and touching Angela on the sleeve. She could feel the woman shaking beneath her fingertips.

"I'm…I'm fine," Angela whispered fiercely. "I shouldn't have called you in here. It's just that I wanted you to know that I'm not as hard as I seem most of the time. I like you and that adorable little son of yours. I didn't want to leave with you still thinking that I was trying to steal Spencer from you. If I had known…well, who am I kidding? If I had known, I would have come anyway. I guess I'm weaker than I thought."

Kate almost smiled. "I have the feeling that if you were weak, Connor wouldn't be arguing with you. You always seem pretty formidable to me. It's admirable to stand so tall when things are working out so badly for you."

Angela let out something that sounded like a sob that turned into a chuckle. "I hope you lead the Fairfields on a merry dance, Kate," she said, turning around and surprising Kate with a hug. "Except Loretta. I love Loretta. She means so well. Make her happy, Kate. I know that Spencer brought you here to make her happy. Do it."

Kate could only hug Angela back and nod. She couldn't pack her own bags and depart even though that was what she wanted to do. She had made a promise. More than once, it seemed. She was here to make Loretta Fairfield's birthday a happy one.

And she couldn't leave until she'd done that.

Fifteen minutes later, Angela pulled away from the door in a Fairfield limousine.

And Kate steeled herself to figure out how she could appear to be involved with Spencer for the next few days while still protecting herself from the raw emotions he called up in her.

But the decision was taken out of her hands in the following minutes. Spencer appeared at breakfast, freshly shaved, tall and handsome with eyes that melted her through and through.

He smiled at her. "Grandmother, I hope you'll forgive me if I take Kate and Toby off today. There's a children's museum just a short distance away," he explained to Kate. "I thought Toby might enjoy spending a couple of hours there. I have to warn you, though. I hear that it's usually somewhat crowded."

Which would mean that they would be away from here and the pressure to pair them up for life. They would be in a place where there were so many people that the two of them would have no chance of slipping up and touching again. It was as if he had read her thoughts…and her fears.

"Toby loves crowds," she said. A few minutes later when she brought him downstairs, he crowed in delight at the sight of Spencer. Kate felt a sharp tug on her heart. Toby was obviously growing too attached to Spencer.

What could she do about that? she wondered. She'd spent years trying to protect her sister from chasing what she couldn't have. Now she would have to protect her son as well.

Kate wanted to cry, but that was something she never did. Instead, she gave Loretta a hug and waved goodbye to Connor as the two of them waited in the doorway. She thought that both of them looked upset and she wondered if Angela had stopped to say goodbye. To Loretta, certainly, but to Connor?

Kate didn't know, but she did know that Angela wouldn't have wanted her to interfere. She was used to trying to fix things for people, but she'd learned that some things just couldn't be fixed. So she said a silent prayer for Angela's happiness. And then she turned toward the waiting limo.

Spencer was there, and all thoughts of anyone else fled. He was smiling that slow, sexy smile that made her want to do terribly misguided things that she'd never wanted to do before.

"You're a brave lady. Thank you for staying. I wanted to tell you so this morning. Now that we're alone, I can," he said as he took Toby from her and fastened him into his child seat.

She frowned. "You thought I'd bolt?"

"I didn't say that, but I wouldn't have blamed you if you had gone."

"I'm not that chickenhearted." Which was a total lie. She'd practically had to tie herself to the bed to keep herself from running out the door.

"No one ever would accuse you of being cowardly, Kate, but you would have been justified in calling a halt to our deal. I crossed the line."

"That's not fair to you. I'd say we crossed it together. I wanted you, too, you know. I just couldn't—"

His eyes turned dark, he frowned and he placed his fingers on her lips. "You were right not to. I shouldn't have tried to push you in that direction. Maybe if we keep our focus on the lighthearted today, things will be easier.''

She nodded and he helped her into the car. So, he wasn't going to let her shoulder the blame. And he was taking her child to a kids' museum. ''Thank you for thinking of Toby again,'' she said as he joined her and Toby, and the limousine circled the driveway and headed for town.

Spencer grinned. ''Don't think I'm being unselfish. I never really understood just how valuable a baby can be. Gives you all kind of excuses to do things you want to do but would be too embarrassed to indulge in under normal circumstances. You're my ticket in to the world of play, big guy, aren't you?''

Toby bucked in his car seat. ''Play now.''

''Soon,'' Kate said, leaning over to kiss his soft, fuzzy cheek.

No matter what Spencer said, she wasn't falling for that I'm-doing-this-for-me act. He had the money, the looks, the personality and the everything else to do anything he wanted to. If he had truly wanted to play in a children's museum, he could have rented out the place and thrown a party for his friends. Instead, he concentrated on making the day fun for her son. At the museum's minimaze, he reached out for Toby's hand.

''Stay with me, buddy,'' he whispered to Toby as the two of them got down on their knees and prepared to enter the rainbow-colored tunnels. ''We're off on an adventure. Tell your mom we'll meet her on the other side.''

He winked at Kate as the two of them started through the maze. Now and then she caught a glimpse of Spencer watching over her son, guiding him so he wouldn't get lost or scared.

When they emerged a few minutes later, Toby was gazing at Spencer adoringly. "Fun. Again," he said, and Spencer gamely complied. The third time, however, Kate crossed her arms.

"Twice is enough," she said. "I don't want him spoiled."

Spencer shrugged. Toby looked as though he wanted to cry.

"Oh no, buddy. There's more to do. Look over there. Bubble city. Let's try it." And Toby toddled over to the area that had been set up with dozens of bubble-making devices.

The diversion worked, and soon the three of them were happily making bubbles. "Thank you," Kate mouthed over Toby's head.

Spencer smiled back at her. "I'm having a blast. He's a joy. And you've got a bubble caught in your hair." He reached out and gently wiped away the errant suds.

It wasn't much of a touch. She barely felt it, but she knew he had touched her. She suddenly didn't know how to breathe just right.

"I'll try to be more careful," she said.

"Don't be more careful because of me. You're already doing that. It's difficult enough to forgive myself for that."

"Because of *me*," she stressed. "I'm responsible for my own reactions."

His lips twisted up as he shook his head. "So serious. So fair and ever practical, Kate."

"That's me," she said, crossing her arms.

"I wasn't criticizing."

"I know." Still, she had always taken lots of criticism, from her mother and her sister, for being too serious, for not having any fun and always worrying about tomorrow. It was difficult not to be defensive. She wanted to be more fun, she really did, but if she ever truly let go, she might forget the consequences of her actions. Terrible things could happen.

"Look, Toby. Out there. Want to give it a try?" she suddenly heard Spencer ask. Her son must have nodded.

"Good. Get Mom and let's go."

And suddenly her son was staring up at her with those big, limpid blue eyes filled with hope. "Try," he begged, and she knew she would have tried anything.

But she hadn't banked on just what anything was, as Toby pointed out the window. There on the grassy area was a hot-air balloon. "Ride," he told her. "Us." And he reached out his hand to bring Spencer closer.

Kate instantly felt the small claws of panic beginning to emerge. "Oh, I don't think so, sweetie."

Toby looked at the balloon and back to her. "Pease," he said.

And then Spencer was by her side. "You're trembling," he said. "I hadn't thought. I'd actually forgotten, but...don't worry. I'll take him up alone. If that's all right?"

Would it be all right for someone else to do something for her son that she was afraid to do?

"It's so silly to be afraid of heights. It doesn't even look like they take you up that far," she said, but her heart still rose in her throat.

"It's not silly. Lots of people feel the way you do."

"I'm coming with you."

"And have me feel guilty forever after for terrorizing you?"

She frowned at him. "This is my choice. Toby is my son. I don't want him acting like this when he grows up."

"Maybe, but this could have waited a few years if I had taken the time to remember a few important things."

The fact that he remembered at all touched her. "No time like the present," she managed to whisper. "Face your fears and all that." But a part of her knew she was all talk. She just didn't want to look like a coward in front of Spencer.

"All right then." Spencer gazed into her eyes. "You are one stubborn lady, Kate. You know that?" And he bent and kissed her. Quickly. "If you have to worry about something, worry about that."

But instead of worrying her, his kiss calmed her, warmed her. And *that* worried her.

Still, he was right. All that thinking about his kiss allowed her to at least move her feet when they had been frozen in place just a second before. And without another word, Spencer shepherded her and Toby aboard the balloon. "Into your mother's arms," he directed her son, picking him up and settling him into her embrace.

He nodded to the balloonist, who nodded back. The balloon began to rise into the sky. Kate fought her panic, and she hoped she wasn't squeezing Toby too tightly. She was embarrassed to find that her eyes automatically closed as the balloon rose.

"Steady, sweetheart," Spencer whispered, and his arms came around her and Toby, pulling them close.

Almost instantly the fear of falling faded a bit. She wasn't completely calm, but she knew without question that Spencer would not let her or her child fall. He would protect them if they were in peril.

"You okay, Toby?" he asked near her ear.

"Good," Toby agreed.

"You all right?" Spencer whispered into her hair.

She managed to smile. "Well, I'm in the air and I'm still alive. I'm all right," she whispered back, turning her head slightly. Her lips ended up much too close to Spencer's and she instantly turned back around before she could do something that would spoil the ride.

"Thank you," she said. "Thank you very much."

And his arms tightened around her almost imperceptibly. She felt like sighing...or crying. But she wouldn't spoil the day with tears. This time would never come again.

Spencer's grandmother's birthday was only two days away.

"He's so full of life," Loretta Fairfield said to Kate that afternoon. She watched Toby as he jumped from one black square on the marble-tiled floor to the next one. "I love it. Makes the rest of us look bad."

Kate smiled at her. "Oh, I'd say you're still pretty full of life yourself."

She was surprised to see a sad look on Loretta's face. "No, no, I don't feel full of life. I feel old. Maybe even used up."

"You miss Angela."

Loretta shrugged. "Yes, but it's more than that. I feel as if I failed her."

"Because of Spencer?"

Loretta's lips turned up slightly. "You're smarter than that, Kate. Did you really think I didn't see?" Her intense blue eyes stared into Kate's, and Kate wondered what else Loretta knew.

"Because of Connor then," Kate said.

The older woman sighed. "We Fairfields are so stubborn. We only love once, you know. Be careful of him, Kate."

Kate knew what she meant. She could have told her that there was nothing to fear for Spencer, but that wouldn't have been fair and it wouldn't have made Loretta feel any better, anyway. It would have only spoiled her birthday more than it was already being spoiled by the day's circumstances.

"What did you and your husband like to do best?" she asked suddenly.

Loretta chuckled. "Trying to distract me? All right then, I'll play along. Other than making love, we liked to dance. He was such a romantic dancer. Rhumbas, tangos, twirls and dips."

"And don't you dance anymore?"

"Me? At my age? Don't be silly." There was something in her voice that brooked no argument, but there for a moment, Kate had noticed a light in her eyes. It was that light that had Kate doing what she knew she shouldn't do.

Spencer wasn't difficult to locate. Every pretty young maid in the house seemed to know where he was. Kate found him in the library.

When he looked up from the book he was perusing and focused on her, Kate felt her heart trip itself up.

Just like magic, it happened every time. He stood and smiled, and she could barely breathe. "Were you looking for me, Kate? May I help you?"

She raised her chin. "Your grandmother's party, is there—do you think there will be dancing?"

His eyes began to twinkle. "I haven't a clue. She plans it all herself, you know. It's an issue with her. But there never has been dancing before. At least not in many years. Is dancing important?"

"I think it may be, yes."

"Care to share your reasoning with me or do you simply like to dance?" He held out his arms as if he planned to waltz with her, and she felt her cheeks turn to flame.

"I—I really don't dance," she stammered, "but your grandmother used to. When your grandfather was alive. She doesn't anymore."

"I see."

"I don't think she's very happy right now. She's worried about you and your brother."

"She always is."

"Yes, but now that Angela's gone, she's worried more, and I have a feeling that she isn't completely fooled by you and me."

"I've suspected that for a while. It's a problem."

"Yes."

"One we could deal with, but I don't want to put you through what I've already put you through in order to alleviate her fears. I don't want to build up the intensity publicly when I'm not completely impervious to you."

She shook her head. "I'm not worried about you falling in love with me. You said you wouldn't."

"And you said that you weren't going to fall in love with anyone, either."

"I won't," she insisted both to him and to herself.

"But I am very attracted to you, Kate. You know that."

"I'm sure it's temporary," she assured him.

A smile flitted across his face, but it didn't touch his eyes, and then those eyes darkened. "I lust for you, Kate. That's dangerous business for two people who want to keep their distance."

She thought it was beyond dangerous business. In spite of her flippant words, she knew danger every moment she was with Spencer. She trusted him, but herself? Absolutely not.

"We won't dance then, you and me," she said, "but I think we should still see if we can have music and dancing. Your grandmother really needs a lift. I'm happy that she's so enamored of Toby, but it's probably not healthy for her to get too attached to him or to concentrate her energies only on him, since we'll be leaving soon. Or even on you and your brother, since neither of you appears to be willing to…"

Her hands fluttered as she searched for the right words.

"Buy into the family curse?" he suggested. "Sacrifice our souls on the altar of love and marriage?"

"I suppose that's not a bad way of putting it."

He chuckled. "So you think we need dancing."

She braved her fears and gazed directly into his eyes. "I think we at least have to try to arrange something to cheer Loretta up."

"Kate," he whispered, stepping closer to frame her face with his hands. "What did this family do to deserve you? You've been much too good to us. This isn't even your battle.''

"Your grandmother has been kind to Toby and me. You've been kind. And I feel guilty for deceiving her.''

"Do you really think she's deceived?''

"No, not at all, but she knows we're not living the truth.''

"And what is the truth, Kate?''

She reached up and claimed his hands, though touching him cost her a heart that would not be still. "You know the truth. I'm here only for convenience. You hired me to make your grandmother's birthday a bit brighter and I agreed so that my son would finally have a week of freedom to really be a child and so that a bunch of disadvantaged children could have something better out of life. This is a deal. I want to do my part of it and not just because it's a job I signed on for. Your grandmother has been a bonus for Toby and me. She's welcomed us into her home even though I'm sure she suspects something of the truth. We can't change what's happened with Angela and we can't provide Loretta with a wife for you, so let's make things as nice for her as we can.''

He brushed his thumbs gently across her cheeks. "I'll see what I can do,'' he whispered.

She nodded and slipped free of his grasp, pivoting toward the door.

"Kate?''

She turned around again.

"Just one dance. After all, we don't have to worry about Fitz objecting.''

It was impossible to keep from smiling. "No, I

guess we don't, but I told you, I never really learned to dance.''

''But you used to try.''

She was sure she was blushing. ''That little girl disappeared a long time ago. I never got the steps down right, and I gave up dancing. Too impractical.''

''And yet you want me to hire a band so my grandmother can dance.''

''Well…yes, I do.''

''Stubborn woman,'' he said with a grin. ''I'll do it, but I'll demand one dance as a boon.''

She smiled and shook her head. ''Stubborn man.''

''Aren't you going to plant your hands on your hips and deny me my rights the way you used to do when we were children?''

''I never denied you your rights. I only demanded mine.''

''I know. You wanted to get married, among other things. You were magnificent. One dance, Kate. My grandmother will think it strange if we hire a band and then don't show up on the dance floor together.''

Ah, he'd caught her there.

''Completely stubborn man,'' she clarified. ''Unfortunately it's difficult to argue with you when you're right. One dance, but don't blame me if I damage your toes by stepping on them.''

He grinned. ''How can I blame you? You've done what no one has ever done before. You've taken part of the planning of Loretta Fairfield's birthday party out of her hands. She's very proprietary about it, you know. I can't wait to see the results.''

''Will she be angry, do you think?''

''Who can tell?''

She raked her lower lip with her teeth. ''Perhaps I

was wrong to suggest it. Maybe it wasn't such a good idea.''

But he moved forward and slipped his hand around her waist. He gave her one quick twirl around the floor as he smiled into her eyes. ''No chance I'm backing out now. You've planted the seed of an idea and I intend to see it through. Beware the dangers of handing an intriguing proposition to a Fairfield, Kate. We tend to be a bit single-minded once we decide to do something.''

''Like buying me at the auction?''

''Definitely like that.''

She stared into his eyes, breathless, his hand still resting on her waist. ''I'll try to be more careful from now on.''

''Yes. Do.''

''Perhaps I shouldn't have told you about Fitz not being real. I think I liked the idea of having a pretend fiancé.''

''I liked it, too, but you don't have one any longer, Kate. For better or for worse, you are a free woman. You make your own decisions.''

Yes, she did. She always had, but why oh why, when she was close to Spencer, did she feel as if she was constantly in danger of deciding to make the same kinds of stupid decisions that her mother and sister had made?

Chapter Nine

Spencer woke late that night with Kate on his mind. Again. It was getting to be a bad habit.

"And why not? She's a beautiful woman and it seems she's also unattached," he muttered to himself, sitting up halfway to gaze out the window by his bed. Plenty of stars this evening. He wondered if Kate had seen them or if she was asleep. For one crazy moment he considered tapping on her door and inviting her out onto the lawn to lie back and count the constellations the way they had once on one long distant night before.

"Hell, Fairfield. Give it a rest," he said, falling back against the pillows. Why was the woman so much on his mind? She was beautiful, but he'd had beautiful.

Maybe it was just this morning at the museum, the utter rightness of the situation. A man, a woman, a child, and none of the complications he eschewed. He didn't want love, *she* certainly didn't want love. That was definitely a plus.

Furthermore, Kate had other good points. She was a person who was kind to his grandmother and she tolerated his brother's bad moods. Her needs were simple: room and freedom for her son, her own escape from her lovelorn boss's pursuit.

There was something else about Kate, too.

He desired her. Completely. Constantly.

A plan began to form in his mind, one that would solve both their problems, make his grandmother happy and relieve him of the dilemma he had lived with all his life.

It wouldn't do to start anything yet, not with the house in an uproar over the coming celebration. Kate was stressed enough. But as soon as that was past, he would approach her.

"It's a reasonable idea. Kate's a reasonable woman. Surely she'll agree."

Kate rose later than usual the day of the party and found that a maid had already taken her son downstairs to feed him. What kind of a mother did that? Ordinarily Toby never woke up without her hearing him, but lately she hadn't been sleeping well. It was as if she guarded herself against getting too entangled with Spencer, even in her dreams.

At least she wouldn't have to worry about that much longer. Her task here was almost done. If she danced with Spencer at the party, that would be the last time she'd be in his arms.

Thank goodness, just one more day of guarding against temptation. Perhaps she should spend today in her room. With all the preparations going on, she might not be missed.

But as she passed the parlor on the way to the breakfast room, Kate heard the sound of laughter. She stuck her head in the doorway and saw Spencer's grandmother sitting on the sofa watching Toby and Spencer and Connor playing together. Connor looked up at that moment from a tall structure he had made from blocks, and she noted for the first time that when he smiled he looked practically boyish. How often did he smile? she wondered.

As for Spencer, he was kneeling on the floor, his attention centered on guiding Toby's little fingers in fastening two blocks together. Her son made the connection with Spencer's help, then looked at the man who had been so patient with him.

"You're pretty good at this, little man," Spencer said. "This building you and Connor are making is a beaut."

"Boot?"

"Absolutely," Spencer agreed. And as if he had felt her presence, he looked up just then. His sleeves were pushed up to the elbows, showing firm muscles and tanned skin. His hair had fallen over his forehead in a way that made Kate itch to sink to her knees, reach out and brush it back.

He smiled suddenly. "Ah, we've been caught, Toby, my boy. There's Mom. See?"

Toby turned in a rush with a smile on his face. "Mom. Toys."

"I see," she said. "Different ones than you've been playing with, too. I haven't seen those before."

Loretta chuckled. "No, they were Spencer's. He went up into the attic this morning with Connor and brought them down."

Spencer tossed a block in the air and caught it with a shrug. "Everyone else is getting a little excitement today with the party going on. I just thought maybe Toby could use something to rev up his day, too. Besides, Connor and I can always use a little fun, and you can never have too many toys."

"Maybe, but I don't want him to get spoiled," Kate said.

Spencer cocked his left eyebrow. "He's not spoiled, Kate."

No, he wasn't, and right now Toby was beaming. He sat down in the middle of the pile of blocks and the wooden train set and simply looked happy gazing at all the toys and the two men who flanked him.

"And he's not hurting anything," Spencer added. "If these were breakable, Con and I would have wrecked them long ago, but, I suppose you're right. I should have asked your permission."

"No, I'm sorry. I'm grateful," she said softly. She had only been perverse because this gesture touched her so much and she didn't want Spencer to do any more nice things for her son.

"Still, you're his mother. You get to say yes or no. I'll ask before I act in the future."

But they both knew that this was the only future. Tomorrow she and Toby would be off. And there would be no man to notice that her son needed diversion on a day when the house would soon be bustling and no one might notice a child's simple needs.

Hours later, Kate opened her door to find Spencer waiting to escort her downstairs for the celebration. She'd already tucked Toby into his bed.

"You look exquisite," he said, standing back to look at her ice-green dress with the tiny capped sleeves that almost bared her shoulders. "Beautiful. No little girl with dirt on her chin, a Wonder Woman T-shirt and skinned knees tonight, eh, Kate? Although that look was just as impressive in its own way."

She looked up into those sapphire eyes that always made her feel as if he saw beyond the outfit to her soul. Even when they had been very young, Spencer had noticed too much.

"I'm a different person than I was then," she said softly. "And so are you."

"Yes," he said. "No more superhero stuff for me, either." She could have argued that point, because he was very much mistaken, but this was a night for celebrating, not debating.

"I hope your grandmother has a wonderful birthday. I understand that even more relatives showed up today."

"Yes, the Fairfields come out of the woodwork for this annual event. Unfortunately some of them come for less than noble reasons, mostly to catch up on the family gossip. Connor and I don't make it easy for Grandmother. She would love to be able to tell everyone she was expecting a great-grandchild."

His deep voice resonated through her, and Kate found she couldn't keep looking into his eyes. Her heart pounded too hard when she was this close. Her thoughts ceased to make sense. She was far too aware of herself as a woman and of Spencer as a man. Especially tonight, when she would have to say goodbye to Spencer. She hoped she had the presence of mind to do it right, lightly and with a smile and good cheer.

She was going to miss him, she finally admitted. His smile, his eyes, the way he treated her son. So many things.

But she couldn't let herself think about that now. Kate pushed her shoulders back. "Shall we get to it?"

He chuckled. "We're not going into battle, Kate."

"No?" she asked with a laugh. "Don't tell me that those curious relatives you spoke of won't be looking at us under a microscope. They'll be looking for chinks in the armor. For your grandmother's sake, I don't intend to let them find any."

He ran one long finger gently down her cheek. "You're really not so different from that little girl, you know."

She opened her mouth to object, but he shook his head. "I admired you then for your ferocious tenacity and your spirit. I still do. You have fire in you, Kate. Wonderful fire. Let's go show everyone what we're made of, shall we?"

Everything was so beautiful, Kate had to admit as they entered the ballroom. Loretta was glowing. The whole room was decorated with flowers and light. The night felt as if it were outlined in gold. Many nights from now she would remember the scent of gardenias, the sparkle of crystal chandeliers, the frothy exotic gowns and the men in their white-on-white tuxes.

Spencer insisted that Kate join him and Connor in standing beside Loretta in the receiving line. She soon realized why as Spencer deftly deflected all questions concerning their relationship, only telling everyone that Kate was a very special friend of his. He beamed down at her each time, and Kate wished she had a glass of water. The room seemed terribly warm.

When the last guest had gone, Spencer disappeared for a few moments and then he led a string quartet to a corner of the room he had commandeered for that purpose.

Loretta turned to her grandsons. "Music? And dancing? Oh, my dears, what a lovely thought."

"Not our lovely thought, however, Grandmother," Spencer said. "Thank Kate. She wanted you to dance."

"Oh, I'm too old."

"Nonsense, Grandmother," Connor said, holding out his arms as the first strains of music flowed into the room. "Let's show them how it's done, shall we?"

The two of them moved onto the floor. Spencer held out one hand.

"My dance, Ms. Ryerson, I believe," he said, sliding his hand to her waist, taking her into his arms and swaying her into the waltz.

Kate stumbled slightly. "I'm sorry. I told you that I wasn't a dancer."

But he only smiled, lifting her slightly off her feet, and moving her back into the rhythm of the dance. "You're many things, Kate, but never a quitter. Ignore your feet, angel. Just enjoy the music and move with me," and he pressed his palm more firmly to her, effortlessly guiding her through the steps. As if she didn't have a choice, she followed his lead.

A thrill ran through her. "You must be very good," she whispered. "I've certainly never danced like this."

"Then shame on the men who partnered you. You should be held in a man's arms often. You're made for movement."

She looked up into his eyes as the room whooshed past in a blur. She wasn't even sure she heard the music anymore. The world was centered in Spencer's hands where he touched her, and in his eyes, which she couldn't look away from. It was as if her feet had disappeared completely and she was simply light, floating in the arms of the man who held her.

All too soon the music slowed to a stop. Spencer bowed over her hand. "Thank you for the dance, Kate. That's a lovely dress, by the way."

She glanced down at the pale green silk that flowed away beneath her breasts. The cut of her gown was lower than she was used to wearing, the tops of her breasts curving softly above the material. She'd been half-afraid to wear it. Now she knew why. The dress made her more aware of her body, especially whenever Spencer looked at her.

"Your grandmother helped me pick it out the other afternoon when we drove into town."

"Ah, I see. Grandmother certainly has incredible taste…and a talent for knowing what men like," he said with a smile that brought a surge of warmth to her cheeks, "but somehow I thought it might be red."

She blinked. "That was a silly little girl who told you that someday she would dance in a long red dress. I don't have the personality for red."

"No?"

"No," she said firmly. Red meant that a person wanted to be a little outrageous, bold and daring. Red was a person who wanted to fight dragons and live on the edge, and who might look into a man's eyes and see possibilities that didn't exist.

"So you don't really like the dress," she said, "but of course, you wouldn't say that. You're far too polite."

He chuckled. "The dress is driving me wild and so is the woman wearing it. I was teasing you, Kate. The color doesn't really matter." But she didn't quite believe him. Spencer would always say the right thing. After all, he protected women and small children. He wouldn't dream of hurting her feelings.

And he would be equally courteous when she took her leave later, she thought as the party took off in earnest and Spencer was called away to play host to some new guests.

Hours later, in need of air, Kate moved to the open French doors leading to the patio.

"Another success for the Fairfields." Connor's voice sounded just behind her.

Kate stepped out to join him beside a rose-filled planter.

"Grandmother will be happy," he said. But Connor didn't sound happy.

"Would you deny her this special day?"

He sucked in a breath. "Of course not. She deserves happiness and more. It's just that this one day always emphasizes what she's waiting for. For Spencer and me to make her truly happy."

"To marry and start a family."

"Yes."

"You're not going to, are you?"

"I won't need to. Spencer intends to. The line will go on."

Yes, Spencer had told her that he would marry,

Kate thought, ignoring the pain that began deep in her chest.

"Someone hurt you once," she said.

He blinked and frowned. "Someone just opened my eyes. Not that they shouldn't have already been open. Spencer may have mentioned our father. He was a strong man once. Never again after my mother died. He didn't even know that Spencer and I existed most of the time. And look at Grandmother. She lives her life waiting for one of us to carry on the Fairfield way. The rest of her life ended when my grandfather went into the grave. She visits there almost daily, you know. Still."

"But Spencer said that you once believed."

He gave an ugly chuckle. "Well, there was a woman willing to disabuse me of the notion of love. All I needed was one sting to realize that I didn't want the ultimate wound. At least I wasn't as deeply involved as I might have been."

"Was it Angela?"

He turned accusing eyes on her. "Angela is none of your business. Or mine, for that matter."

Kate felt color flare in her cheeks. "You're right, of course. I seem to have lost all sense of perspective tonight. I'm sorry."

Connor blew out a breath. "And I seem to have forgotten my manners completely. I know that you asked out of concern, but don't be worried, Kate. We Fairfields can't be saved. And don't feel sorry for *me*. As the younger son, I at least have a choice. Spencer will be the sacrificial lamb. It will fall to him to carry on the line." And he gave her a polite bow and moved away, headed for his grandmother. In a few moments, she saw him dancing with Bridget, who looked thoroughly disgruntled. Loretta was on the floor with Spencer. It was a good time to try to make her escape for a short while.

Kate headed toward the library and a deep couch where she could gather her thoughts and prepare for the end of the evening when she would have to smile despite her impending loss. She liked the Fairfields. She wanted to see them happy, and it was going to be difficult to say goodbye in the morning, knowing that none of them had much hope for happiness.

She tried not to think about what Connor had said about Spencer being the sacrificial lamb. He'd sworn off love, but he would marry someday. He would have children. She would read about it in the newspapers.

And that would be all.

Spencer stepped into the library where a maid had told him she'd last seen Kate. He shut the heavy door behind him and smiled at what he saw.

A lone light on a mahogany book table cast a golden glow on the nearby stacks of books and the dark polished wood. There, on the burgundy brocade sofa Kate lay, her head resting on the arm, her eyes closed. She had slipped off her shoes and curled her feet up beneath the floor-length skirt of her gown. Long, dark lashes brushed her pale skin. Her neck was leaning at what had to be an uncomfortable angle.

Spencer frowned. He hated to wake her, but she would surely pay for her awkward pose with a horrible stiff neck in the morning. For a moment he considered lifting her into his arms and carrying her to her bed, but no doubt they would be seen in the hall and people would comment. Knowing Kate, she would feel guilty at what she perceived as neglecting her duty.

Not that that argument would fly with him. She'd done more than her share this week, tending to his family with a care that went above and beyond what he had asked for. For suggesting the band and the dancing alone he could kiss her. That small gesture had made his grandmother's eyes light with joy. And Kate had stood there for hours this evening conversing with people who no doubt were asking personal questions, or, knowing his relatives, trying to bore her to tears. She had smiled through all of it and tended to small concerns of the staff when he hadn't been on hand to do so. Her rest had been earned.

And she would have it.

He dropped to one knee before her, gently stroking his index finger down her cheek. "Kate," he whispered. "Wake up and let me take you to bed."

She moaned softly in her sleep. She licked her lips, nearly making him groan, but he couldn't keep from smiling. Even dead to the world, Kate was one potent armful.

"Kate," he tried again, moving his lips to her ear. "It's time to go upstairs." His mouth touched her skin, the errant tendrils of silky hair that lay against her cheek. "Shall I carry you and tell the world to go to hell then?"

And he began to slide his hands beneath her. But just as he was about to pull her toward him, she opened her eyes and gasped, sitting straight up. Her actions caught Spencer off balance, and, sliding backward, he took Kate with him. In seconds he was seated on the floor with an armful of Kate held close. Her skirts drifted down around them.

"Spencer?" she whispered as she came fully awake. "What happened? Oh no, I can't believe I did this to you. I can't believe I fell asleep. Is it over? Did anyone notice I was gone? Is your grandmother very upset that I wasn't there to say goodbye to the guests?"

Her hands were resting on his shoulders as she braced herself. Troubled deep-green eyes stared into his own. She shifted, trying to get more comfortable, and he groaned deep in his throat.

"Don't move, Kate. No," he said firmly as she started to shift again and scamper off him. "Just… sit…still. Very still, and we'll talk."

"Yes, but—"

"Shh. Everything's all right. The party isn't over. You can't have been asleep for more than a few minutes. I feel guilty enough that we've worn you out so much that you're exhausted."

"But I'm not—"

He gently touched her lips with two fingers.

"Everything's fine."

She sighed. "I'm glad then. We should go back. Your grandmother will wonder where we are."

He smiled. "You know she'll be delighted if she thinks we're alone somewhere. And she's happy tonight, Kate. Happier than I've seen her in a long time. Thanks to you."

And as if a miracle had happened, she settled herself more firmly against him, trusting him. Didn't she know what her body, pressed against his, was doing to him? He didn't think she did, she was that preoccupied. Or maybe she was just that innocent. The thought both angered him and delighted him. She knew no other man's touch.

"I'm so glad things worked out," she said. And then she smiled right into his eyes.

He knew then that he was going to do something rash. He was not going to consider the ramifications of the action he'd been mulling over for the past few days. Neither was he going to wait and let this moment slip away.

"Let's get married, Kate," he said.

Chapter Ten

Kate's body went hot, then cold, then hot again. She felt as if there was a roaring in her ears. Perhaps she had heard wrong.

"Marry you?" She barely got the words out in a breathless rush.

His fingers tightened on her skin. "Yes. Marry. Oh, I know what you're thinking. If you were standing instead of sprawled deliciously across my body, you'd have your hands planted on your hips. You'd be asking me if I hadn't heard you right when you told me that you wanted nothing of love, but I'm not talking that kind of marriage, Kate. I wouldn't do that to you. I certainly wouldn't wish it on myself."

"But you want to get married."

"I think I do. And why not? Look at us. We've been living in close quarters for a week. We've gotten to know each other's families. What's more, Toby is just the kind of son a man wants, Kate, and I think you feel at least a bit of kinship with my grandmother and Connor, don't you?''

''Yes, of course, but still…'' That tightness in her chest was increasing. She knew she should be objecting more strongly, maybe even inventing a few good reasons why this wouldn't work. But the creative part of her brain seemed to have frozen. In fact all of her seemed to be operating in slow motion, except the part of her that kept repeating the words ''Marry me, Kate. Marry me, Kate.''

''It makes so much sense,'' he coaxed, ''and I know you're very sensible. We can have what we want and not have to worry about the emotional complications that most marriages have. Beyond that, I can give you things, Kate. Not just money. I know that doesn't mean much to you, but it does help now and then. I can give Toby a home, one where you don't have to worry about the landlord complaining when your son runs or makes the kinds of noises that children are bound to make. I can give him stability and security. I can give that to you, too, Kate. We've been good as partners together, haven't we?''

Deep longing began to sift into her consciousness. She nodded slowly. ''We've been very good,'' was all she could say.

''Kate, I need a wife, and you need security. With a real ring on your finger and a real husband, you would never again have to worry about any man harassing you. You wouldn't have to worry about tomorrow or even the details of today. I could take care of everything for you. All you'd need to do would be to concentrate on Toby and yourself.''

''And what will you get in having me as a wife, Spencer?''

He thought about that a minute. "A friend, a companion, a partner, a mother for our children. I'd want it to be real in that respect, Kate. I want you, you know."

She swallowed hard as she looked into his eyes. "Thank you," she said primly.

He chuckled. "I don't think you're completely immune to me, either, are you? Tell me now if I'm wrong."

She couldn't speak. The thought of making children with Spencer made her heart thunder perilously. She shook her head.

"You don't want me, then, Kate?" His voice was low, maybe even a little rough. How could he even think that? He must know it wasn't true.

She shook her head harder, sending strands of her hair floating down around her shoulders. "I'm not completely immune to you," she managed to say.

"Thank all that is glorious in life," he said, and he cupped his hands around her shoulders and pulled her to him in a quick hard kiss.

The door opened at that moment. Kate raised her head and looked at Spencer. She turned to the door where Connor, Loretta and several other relatives were gathered.

"Oh, there you are, dear," Loretta said, her voice perfectly calm and satisfied. "I should have known that Spencer would be doing something productive and highly intelligent."

Spencer placed his lips near Kate's ear. "You know this is a solution to our dilemmas. Say yes, Kate."

She pulled back slightly, staring directly into his eyes. Then, with a deep breath, she closed her mind to the objections that she knew would surely be circling around there if she only gave them a chance for her attention.

"Yes," she said softly.

"Yes, what?" Connor asked.

Spencer stared up at his brother. He looked to his grandmother. "I hope you'll offer us your congratulations. Kate has just agreed to be my bride."

Loretta Fairfield closed her eyes for a second before offering a triumphant, "Thank goodness. I thought it might never happen. That is, I hoped, but…thank you, my dears. This is the perfect birthday present. A fairy-tale wedding," she said, using the word that Kate had avoided all her life.

Kate managed to smile weakly at Loretta. She didn't have the heart to tell her the truth about this marriage. It wasn't to be real, just practical.

But remembering what it felt like to be in Spencer's arms with his lips pressed to hers, Kate knew there would be parts of the marriage that would be less than practical.

They were to share a bed.

The very thought of making love with Spencer made her feel flushed and bothered…and more things that she didn't want to think about. And weren't those the very things that she had been running from all her life?

Getting Kate to agree to marry him had let loose a whirlwind in every sense of the word, Spencer thought a week later. His grandmother had immediately moved into action, asking them to please set a date and allow her to help organize the ceremony since Kate had no immediate family.

"I don't see why she shouldn't," Kate told him. "I've never dreamed of planning a wedding. I wouldn't know the first thing about it and would probably make a horrible mess of things to boot. And it would mean so much to her."

So they had agreed on a date just one month into the future. Kate had placed herself in his grandmother's hands, and that had almost been the last he'd seen of her. Weddings, it seemed, took a great deal of work involving the bride and not the groom.

He had plenty of time to think about the fact that Kate had said that the wedding would mean a great deal to his grandmother.

But not to Kate, he couldn't help thinking.

"So deal with it, Fairfield," he told himself. "You don't want it to mean too much, anyway, do you? You don't want to get deeply involved, and you don't want Kate getting sucked into the very kind of thing that scares her to death, do you?"

No, he didn't want Kate being forced to do anything she didn't want to do, and there lay the gist of the problem.

He had caught her when she'd barely been awake. He had waited until his entire family was crowded around waiting for something to happen before he had urged Kate to give him an answer. She had been cornered, he had pushed her, and as a businessman, he knew how to push.

That's why, now and then, when he saw Kate from a distance and noted the slightly panicked look in her eyes, he wondered what he had done to her. What kinds of wheels had he set in motion and what should he do now?

But he did nothing. He hadn't lied when he told

Kate that he thought they'd suit admirably. He simply didn't like the methods he'd used. In the end, he would still have asked her. He most likely still would have pushed. The end result would have been the same.

For Kate was eminently practical, and this engagement made all kinds of sense.

"And you'd damn well be satisfied with that," he told himself. "She's given you all she can give."

Of course, he didn't want more. He had never wanted more than a convenient marriage with a companionable wife.

But he wanted this to be right for Kate, too. Her needs were more important than his.

So when he saw her hurrying past later that day, he fell into step with her.

"What is it today?" he asked.

She sighed. "A meeting with the florist. He wants to see what flower I remind him of."

A chuckle escaped him. "Want to play hooky? Maybe steal Toby away? There's a badminton court on the west side of the lawns, and I know where Roberts hides the equipment. Even if Toby's too young to play properly, he can have a great time batting a shuttlecock around. And we might convince Connor to slip away from work and come along. He was always fierce competition, and I have the feeling he wouldn't be averse to letting out some pent-up frustration. Setting up a temporary office here makes sense but it steals a lot of his time. He needs a distraction."

Kate glanced longingly toward the area of the property he had indicated, but she shook her head. "I'd like to help Connor, too, but I can't."

"I can promise you sunshine," he whispered.

"Don't do that."

"Green grass. The freedom to run. No one wanting to know what type of flower you resemble."

And with that, she let out a deep sigh and covered her face with her hands. "All right." Her voice came out muffled through her fingertips. "You've caught me. I'm weak."

"You? Weak? Never. You've just been pushed to the limits of your endurance. You need exercise, time to call your own, you need—"

"Is there a red racket, do you think? If there is, I want it," she asked, breaking in. He saw a trace of twinkling green eyes peering over her fingertips.

"I'm sure there is," he said with a grin. "I seem to recall you trouncing me with a racket that color."

And she looked at him wide-eyed. "You're not saying that I'm trying to gain a psychological edge, are you, Fairfield?"

"I'm not saying it. I'm thinking it," he said with a slow smile. "But I stepped right into it, so I deserve whatever happens next. Come on, let's go find Connor and Toby."

He took her hand and pulled her toward the nursery.

She probably shouldn't have capitulated to Spencer's coaxing, Kate thought a few minutes later as she knelt by her son and gave him a nylon shuttlecock to play with. "No feathers for you. You might choke on them," she said as he fingered the scratchy nylon. "Now come with Mom. You can be my partner."

"Mom. Me," he said, clearly entranced with the idea of spending time with her. Her heart nearly broke at the thought of how very much she loved him and how much she wanted to protect him and give him a good life.

Enough to marry a man she had no business marrying. The nasty little thought crept in.

"It's just a deal," she muttered to herself. "Nothing all that risky."

"Planning your strategy, Kate?" Spencer asked with a smile as he came up beside her, his very voice causing shivers to run through her body.

"Who needs strategy when we have skill?" she teased, but she barely got the words out, so aware of Spencer was she. How was she going to marry him, make babies with him and maintain even a semblance of normalcy when his smile made her forget how to breathe?

"To make it fair, you play the first half of the match and I'll play the second, but I don't know if we've got a chance. Kate looks like she knows what she's doing, Spence, and it's been years since we partnered up on a badminton court," Connor said. "Besides, Kate and Toby are smaller than either of us, but they look light on their feet." But Kate noticed that while Connor appeared to tease, there was no life in his voice. He'd stayed on after his grandmother's birthday and after Bridget and all the relatives had left, as if he had no heart for returning to the city. Every day he looked even more unhappy. It had been a woman who had done that to him, even though there had been no intent to hurt.

Kate told herself she should be glad she had no such power over Spencer. He was much too intelligent to ever let his emotions get the best of him.

For some reason, she felt as if the sun dimmed somewhat in that moment.

"Kate." Spencer's voice came soft and low as he leaned over her. "Are you all right? We don't have to do this, you know. And Connor was just teasing."

She looked up into those worried blue eyes and wished she could erase his concern.

"Are you trying to get rid of your fiercest competition, Spencer?" she asked with a deliberate smile.

Still he didn't smile. He studied her for long seconds.

She stared back at him, practically begging him to play along. She needed him to acknowledge that everything was still light and easy. If he was worrying about her, it was because she was sending the wrong signals. And if she was sending the wrong signals, it might be because...well, she didn't even want to think about the reasons why.

She held out her racket, the red one. "You can have it if you think it'll bring you luck. I could let you serve first, too, if you'd like." She offered up the feather-tipped shuttlecock.

Finally, he grinned at her. He leaned and placed his lips near her ear, his breath delicious against her skin. "You don't fool me, Kate. I know you're still frazzled by all these plans that have been pushed on you, but I'm willing to play along if it makes you feel better."

Straightening, he winked at Connor. "She thinks the red racket makes her infallible. She doesn't know how ruthless the Fairfield brothers can be, both in business and on the badminton court."

And he was as good as his word, she thought with a sigh of relief. Spencer played to win, at least he made it appear that way. He laughed wickedly when she sent the shuttlecock sailing out of bounds. He let out a loud "yes!" when he took the lead.

But she also noticed that he called a halt now and then so that he or she could wrap their arms around Toby and help him swing a racket, giving the little boy a chance to hit the shuttlecock around. When Connor took over the court, Spencer moved to Kate's side of the net and put Toby on his shoulders so that the little boy could be tall enough to send the shuttlecock over if Spencer stood against the net and Toby threw rather than hit the shuttlecock.

"Good one. That's a point for your side, buddy," Spencer said, counting the illegal point and allowing Kate and Toby to take back the lead. Spencer picked her son up and swung him around in a circle. "That was amazing," he said to Toby.

Connor and Kate exchanged a look.

"Ruthless, isn't he?" she asked with a smile.

"A take-no-prisoners kind of guy," Connor agreed.

"It's not over until it's over," Spencer remarked with a knowing smile as he put Toby down and moved off the court to let Kate and Connor get back to the game.

But apparently it *was* over. Toby suddenly let out a whimper. He held out his finger to Spencer as big fat teardrops slid down his face. "Owie," he said on a sob. "Bug."

And Spencer dropped to the ground and scooped Toby into his arms. "He's been stung by a bee, Kate. He's not allergic, is he?"

She shook her head and joined her son and her husband-to-be on the ground, crooning to Toby. "It's not likely for a first bee sting," she told Spencer, "but let's get him to the house. Don't worry, sweetheart, Mom will make the sting stop soon."

But she wondered how she would make the sting in her heart stop as she watched Spencer soothe her son and cuddle him close on the trip to the house. She realized something right there and then.

Spencer Fairfield was a knight on a white horse even though she didn't want to believe in such things.

What on earth was she going to do about the turn her thoughts were taking?

Nothing. Nothing, she told herself. It's just all nonsense, crazy thoughts brought on by the fact that the wedding plans had robbed her of sleep and sanity.

Spencer was just a man. Their marriage would just be a formality, nothing more. There was nothing to worry about.

Chapter Eleven

There was something very wrong here, Spencer thought nearly a week later. Connor was looking more morose every day, his grandmother was looking more determined and Kate was showing very definite signs of strain. He found himself studying her whenever she entered a room.

She always smiled back, brilliantly, in fact.

Too brilliantly. He was beginning to get the decided feeling that she wanted this marriage to help him, and she wanted this chance for security for her son, but she did not want to be his wife. Was she sacrificing herself for her child and for him? Spencer wondered.

A dull ache began deep inside him. He looked up as Connor came into his office and threw himself into the chair across from his desk.

"I should be going home," Connor said.

"I wondered why you hadn't already. You've been handling your share of Fairfield Limousine from here just as I have, but I have a reason for the extra inconvenience. You don't.''

"Are you sure I don't?''

"What's that supposed to mean?''

"I suppose it means that I'm worried about you.''

Spencer raised his head and studied Connor's expression. Connor was angry. The way he'd been for some time.

Shaking his head, Spencer got up from his chair and sat on the edge of his desk. "You mean because of Kate, don't you? If so, then don't worry. There's nothing to take care of. She and I are both adults and we've chosen to do this thing.''

"I don't think it's that simple.''

"It is,'' Spencer insisted, "and it's our concern, not yours, though I appreciate the fact that you care.''

"You're not immune to your emotions,'' Connor insisted, "much as you try to be. I know. It's a difficult task we've both set ourselves, to remain uninvolved.''

And Spencer felt his own concern rear its head. "I'm just looking for a little contentment and a little closure, Connor. I hope you find the same someday.''

"I see the way you look at her.''

"I look at her the way any man would look at the woman he plans to marry.''

"But you're not just any man. You're a Fairfield. Remember that, Spence. Please remember that.''

And Connor slipped from the room.

Spencer broke the pencil he was holding in his hands. "Weddings certainly are a lot of trouble, aren't they?'' he asked the empty room.

His brother was wrong, of course. There was no danger here, just a man and a woman trying to make a convenient future. Once the marriage had been completed, things would surely settle into mere contentment.

But a vision of Kate smiling up at him drifted through his mind, and the hunger began. He was beginning to worry that Connor might have hit on a shred of truth. Did he want Kate to give him the one thing he had always said he didn't want, the one thing it was impossible for her to give?

Spencer blew out a frustrated and half-panicked breath. The next time he saw Kate he was definitely going to have to analyze his reactions.

And if he couldn't control them, then what?

Kate was avoiding all thoughts of Spencer today—or trying to. She was very aware of that fact.

Well, of course, she thought as she tried to stand patiently for the final fitting of the gown. She had things to do for the wedding and she had to think about what she and Toby were going to do tonight. Her time was taken up.

But no, it was more than that. She'd been talking to Grandmother Fairfield, who'd told her what a charming boy Spencer had been and how much his father had loved his mother. Loretta had related how she had loved her husband and how Spencer would now love Kate.

And every time Loretta mentioned Spencer loving her, Kate ached, more and more. She thought of him hugging her son, teasing her, kissing her. She thought of him worrying about his family. He was such a good man, a handsome and virile man.

A dream man.

Oh, no. She closed her eyes suddenly, trying to retract the thought.

"Stop fidgeting, Kate. You're going to be a mass of pinholes or else that lovely dress is going to get torn."

Kate looked down from the slightly raised platform she was on. Loretta was eyeing her, the gown and the seamstress with concern. If Kate didn't know how happy this marriage was making Loretta, she would almost think some of her own worry had worn off on Spencer's grandmother. Loretta looked a bit tired today.

"Maybe we should finish this another time," Kate offered.

Or never, her aching heart urged her to shout. But she remained silent.

Loretta shook her head vehemently. "I'm afraid we can't. Time is too short, but I am sorry, my dear. Your life has been so busy lately. I'm glad that you at least got to slip out with Spencer to attend that dinner with his friends, Ethan and Dylan, and their companions. And soon the wedding will be over. You and Spencer will be married and off on your honeymoon."

The very thought of going on a honeymoon with Spencer made Kate take in too deep a breath, and she failed to suppress her gasp when her movements did bring a pin up against her skin.

"Grandmother, are you torturing my bride?" Spencer's deep voice came from the open doorway.

"Spencer, you're not supposed to be here. You can't see Kate in her wedding gown."

But he kept moving, coming closer to her, his eyes all dark blue and focused on her. Kate swallowed convulsively as she twisted the Fairfield emerald on her finger. "You look ready to collapse, angel," he said softly. "Why don't we steal a few minutes so you can get your breath and rest your legs."

And suddenly Kate wanted nothing more than to take his hand and go with him.

Anywhere. Under any circumstances.

Which meant that she should definitely stay right here.

"I don't think so," she said, shaking her head vehemently.

"I think so."

"Spencer, she can't—" Loretta began, but Spencer stopped her with a look.

"I know how much you're enjoying all the plans, Grandmother, and I'm glad, but Kate isn't used to all the rush and bother of the Fairfields. She lives a more quiet lifestyle, and I think she really needs a few minutes. Badly."

His grandmother looked slightly guilty. "I guess I have been pushing things. It's just that—"

"Shh, there's no need to apologize, Grandmother. I understand."

Kate did, too. It was herself and her reactions to Spencer that she didn't understand.

"I'm grateful for all your help," she told Loretta, determined to ignore Spencer's invitation and stay right where she was. But then he held out his hand.

Such a simple thing, really, but then she made the mistake of looking into his eyes, she leaned toward that smile that turned her insides to cream. And without even thinking, she put out her own hand.

Oh no, don't, she tried to tell herself.

But she stepped down from her perch, placing her hand in his as her senses lurched crazily. Anticipation began to build inside her. Her legs felt wooden. She should not be doing this, following him like a needy pet, willing to do anything just to be near his voice.

But she *was* doing it. Only a small, still-logical part of her brain enabled her to stop herself from walking right into Spencer's arms. That part of her whispered that Loretta was going to be hurt by this defection.

She managed to turn to Spencer's grandmother who was looking at her with anxious eyes. "I know we have to get things done quickly," she said, "and I really am grateful that you've taken care of all the arrangements. If left to my own devices, I'd probably be wearing something hideous. I didn't even know what a Christos gown was. Now that I do, I'm amazed that you managed this so quickly. Thank you."

Loretta turned a soft pink. She fidgeted and then smiled. "Well, if a woman of my ilk can't manage to finagle a designer gown, what can I do? But Spencer is right. You go off and play for a while. Spencer, leave the room. She'll be right with you, and yes, I promise. No more fittings for an hour. I'll just go see if Toby has awakened from his nap."

And less than ten minutes later, Spencer was leading Kate through the house.

"Where are we going?" she asked as if it mattered. As if she wouldn't follow him down to inspect the furnace if that was what he suggested they do.

"We're going to play hooky again," he said, linking his fingers more closely with hers.

"I got that part, but what exactly are we going to do?" Her lips burned, and she tried her best to keep her mind off what she wanted to do with Spencer.

He slowed his pace. "There's a stable down the road where Grandmother keeps horses. Do you ride?"

Her fingers suddenly felt cold against Spencer's warmth. ''Um, no, I'm afraid I haven't been on anything resembling a horse since I rode the ponies at a fair when I was little. And they were just going in an endless circle at turtle speed.''

''Turtle speed, huh? Do you trust me then?''

She gazed up into his eyes. ''I've come here with you, haven't I?'' she whispered.

''Yes, and you've done all that I asked of you,'' he said, stopping to face her and take both her hands in his. ''Then trust me once more. I won't betray that trust.''

But that wasn't what she was afraid of. She was afraid of herself, of betraying *his* trust.

And so she blindly followed him. When he brought out a cream-white horse that tossed its mane and whinnied to Spencer, Kate held her breath, but she didn't let her fear show.

And when Spencer held out his hand, she let him help her mount the horse. Then he swung up into the saddle behind her.

''We'll share,'' he said softly. ''Merlin won't mind. He's very gentle.''

As was Spencer. His arms enfolded her. She breathed in his scent, leaned back into his embrace. The wind lifted her hair and kissed her face as he urged the horse from a sedate walk to a trot.

She was flying, Kate thought, on a horse with a name that recalled the days of noblemen and knights. She was in heaven. But no, she was in Spencer's arms, which felt like heaven.

She squirmed, turning slightly in his arms as she tried to wriggle away from her thoughts.

''Are you all right?'' he asked. ''I just thought we

might chase the cobwebs from your mind, ride away from all the cares of the wedding arrangements and run away for a few hours. I'll take you back soon. We'll play a game with Toby.''

She closed her eyes and lay back, breathing in the scent of leather and man as Spencer's warmth enfolded her.

I would love that, she thought. But as she rested in his arms, held close against his heart, her thoughts caught up to her. She knew that she loved him.

And why wouldn't she? He was a man who had enough wealth and power that he didn't have to think of anyone but himself, and yet he took care of his grandmother, of herself and Toby. He had taken her out of the house today just because he was concerned for her.

And who would be concerned for him? Who would protect him?

She loved him, but she knew that more than anything else he wanted his heart to remain free. Her love would be a burden, one she was sure he would never hold against her but which would weigh him down forever.

He would care for her always, but he would never return her love.

''Or we don't have to play a game,'' he teased when she still hadn't answered him.

Kate felt warm color rising to her cheeks. ''I'm sorry. Playing a game would be nice,'' she said. ''You're very good to us, you know.''

''You're my fiancée, you'll be my wife. Why wouldn't I be?''

But she knew now that she would never be his wife, and she would tell him so just as soon as she had a few minutes to prepare herself and enough time to make up a story that would sound believable. Would anything sound truly believable when she had been trying on her wedding gown only a short time ago?

What could she tell Spencer that wouldn't sound cowardly and as phony as her former fiancé? She didn't know, but she knew that she had to make up for her cowardice in some way.

What could she possibly do that would make a difference?

Kate entered the parlor where Loretta was reading a book. "Do you mind if I have a few minutes of your time?" she asked.

"Well, I've certainly taken up more than a few minutes of yours lately," the woman said, smiling and patting the sofa beside her. "And don't tell me how grateful you are for my help. You know that I'm doing this as much for me as for you."

"All right, I won't say it. I'll just think it."

"What can I help you with?" the other woman asked as Kate sat down. "Is it something about Spencer?"

Kate shook her head. "No, it's something about you. You remember how you told me that you and your husband met Picasso and that you enjoyed art and dancing. I'm…enthralled. Would you mind telling me a bit more about what your life was like?"

The older woman chuckled. "Would I mind talking about the most wonderful years of my life? Kate, I'd love to. I just avoid it so people won't worry that I'm living in the past."

"The past can be important."

"Very important. Well then, let me see…Hugh and I traveled a lot. It was wonderful. We went to the theater, and now and then we even painted together. Hugh was very good at it. I wasn't, but it didn't really matter. I enjoyed it."

"Do you still paint?"

"Oh, my, no. It just never seemed right, without him. We would take our easels and our paints and a picnic basket and make an outing of it. It was more than just painting."

"It sounds so incredibly lovely. Perhaps you should try painting again."

"Alone?"

"Why not? Lots of things are fun alone. They're not the same as they would be with the person you love, but they can be very nice in a different way. Don't you think your Hugh would like to think of you down here painting away and dancing and traveling and going to the theater?"

"Oh yes, of course he would, dear. Hugh always wanted those he loved to be happy."

"Like Spencer."

"I know that, but you don't know how it is with we Fairfields. It just wouldn't seem right doing all those things without Hugh, and besides, I'm content. I have my family."

"And they love you. You're a wonderful, giving person. You should have more of the good things life has to offer. No matter what you do, you'll still have your family and your memories, won't you?"

Loretta chuckled. "Why are you doing this, Kate? Don't tell me that you're starting to worry about me, too."

Kate realized that she was. She wasn't just having

this discussion because of Spencer, but also because Loretta would be hurt when she left without marrying her grandson. And because Spencer's grandmother had become more to her than just a hostess. How could she not care about what happened to Loretta?

"You have so much to give," Kate said. "I really would love to see something you've painted. And yes, I do think that your family would gain something, too. They'd love to see you enjoying yourself."

Loretta reached out and patted her hand.

"You're a treasure, Kate. I worried about Spencer so long, but now I see that he was just waiting for you."

And Kate couldn't restrain herself then. She reached out and gave the old woman a big hug. Then she fled the room, knowing she had probably done more harm than good and caused Loretta to worry.

Still, when Kate had managed to calm down, she found herself outside the temporary office Connor had been using.

"Mind if I come in?" she asked when he answered her knock.

He frowned slightly. "Something wrong?"

"No. Yes, there is. I wanted to ask you a question. A nosy question."

That finally made him smile. "A nosy question. Well, at least you're honest. Ask away. I'll decide if I'm ready to reveal all my secrets."

"It's about Angela."

His smile disappeared. "Off limits."

She shook her head. "When she broke your best friend's heart, it was because she decided not to marry him, wasn't it?"

"I suppose there's no point in answering. You seem to already know the details."

"I don't know much. Just that part and one thing more. She decided not to marry him because she was in love with someone else. It would have been wrong to marry a man knowing that she would only hurt him, wouldn't it?"

He stared at her, his expression unreadable.

"Too easy an answer."

Kate breathed in a shaky breath. "I don't think it was easy for her at all," she said. "I got the feeling that it was the hardest thing she'd ever done. She knew she would hurt her fiancé, and that caused her great pain. She didn't do it lightly. And more than that, she knew that in breaking off the engagement, she could never have the man she did love because he would never forgive her. Under the circumstances, many women might have taken the easy way out and gone through with the wedding. Angela didn't, and she's continuing to pay the price."

He stared at her through dark, anguished eyes.

"Connor, I—"

He held up one hand. "Enough. You've gone too far, even for someone I like as much as I like you."

She opened her mouth again.

"Don't, Kate," he pleaded. "It's too late. It's over."

He was right, she supposed as she nodded and moved away. Some things just couldn't be fixed. It was over, for Connor and Angela and also for Spencer and herself.

The fact that she was hurting so much was proof that Connor was right. Things had happened that could not be undone and, like Angela, she would pay the price for the rest of her life.

There was nothing left to do, so she went upstairs, packed her things, went to the nursery and found Toby. She hugged her child, picked him up and went in search of Spencer.

The page in front of him was covered in doodles when Spencer looked up and saw Kate in the doorway. He had been thinking of her, wishing he could make up some new excuse to steal her away for a few hours, and now she had appeared.

She had Toby with her and a look on her face that would break a man's heart.

"Kate, what's wrong?" he asked, rising and striding toward her. "Come in. Sit down, angel."

"No. I can't. Spencer, we have to talk. We have to…stop."

All coherent thought fled, leaving only a deep sense of panic. "Stop?"

"Yes. I—Spencer, I'm so very grateful for all you've done for me. You've given Toby so much, you've helped a good cause, you've brought me into your family and welcomed me and you were even willing to make me your wife, but—"

"But what?"

She looked away. "But I can't marry you."

For whole seconds, eternities, it seemed, the room was filled with only silence and the little noises Toby was making.

"You can't marry me."

"No." Kate's voice was almost a sob. She still wasn't looking at him.

"I see," Spencer managed to say as panic clawed

its way through his body. He forced himself to take deep breaths.

He reached out and gently took Toby from Kate, hugging the little boy before placing him in the toy-filled playpen he'd installed in his office in recent weeks. Then he turned back.

"Look at me, Kate."

"I want to, but I don't think I deserve to."

"Because you've changed your mind about marrying me?"

"Yes." Her voice was an anguished whisper. She was clearly upset about having to do this. But she shouldn't be. He was the one who had suggested the marriage. He'd practically forced her into it. He'd placed his own needs above hers, and now she wanted out and she was feeling miserable.

He felt much the way he'd once felt when he and Connor had gotten into an all-out brawl and pummeled each other until they could no longer stand. Every part of him stung.

But this was so much worse.

"Kate, are you sure?" He placed one finger beneath her chin and gazed into her tear-filled eyes.

"Shh," he said, kissing her eyelids. "Don't cry."

"I'm not," she insisted as a tear slid down her cheek.

Under other circumstances he would have teased her, but not today, not after this.

"Why?" His voice came out too harsh, like an accusation.

And her eyes opened. She forced herself to look into his eyes. "I was marrying you for the wrong reasons. I wanted things for Toby and myself. A home. Security."

"I know that," he said gently, managing a small smile. "There's nothing wrong with that, you know, Kate. We both agreed that we were marrying for convenience."

"I know," she said, swallowing convulsively, "but that's…that's the problem. I can't—I've decided that I want to marry for love, after all."

Somehow he kept himself from doubling in half with the pain. By some miracle, his knees didn't buckle beneath him. And only by the greatest of mercies did he continue breathing.

"Then you'll do that," he said, forcing his voice to be low and calm and gentle. "There's no doubt in my mind that you'll find the man you're looking for. Most likely someday soon."

He bent and brushed his lips across hers and felt the sweet ache of longing and loss. "Just be happy, Kate. And don't worry about the details of leaving. I'll take care of things."

But she shook her head. "No. I've already done it. I couldn't ask you to do more. My bags are already in a cab." She gazed at him with eyes that were beautiful and haunted. Her lips trembled.

"Spencer," she cried, and she stepped up to him and pressed her lips to his, her tears tasting of salt and regret. "I'm so sorry that it turned out this way. I'm sorry that I'm still that same silly dreamer that I was when we were kids."

She took off her ring and placed it on his desk. Then she picked up Toby and moved toward the door. She left him.

He closed the door and leaned back against it,

sightless, mindless, all pain and nothing more. Except for the refrain that kept running through his head.

He loved her beyond belief. The Fairfield Curse had come looking for him after all, and it had found him.

Chapter Twelve

It was disgusting, Kate thought, gazing out the window for what seemed like the millionth time that day. She kept imagining Spencer riding up to her house on that beautiful white horse, catching her and Toby up into his arms and sweeping away all her arguments about why they couldn't be together.

"Ma, ma." She felt a tugging on her skirt, and Kate looked down to find her son gazing up at her. He was holding a rubber ball in his hand, a hopeful look on his face.

"Oh, sweetie," she said, dropping to her knees and pulling him into her arms. "Of course I'll play with you."

No matter how miserable she felt, no matter if she had turned into a romantic dreamer with no hope of fulfilling those impossible dreams, she must not neglect her child. That was what her mother had done.

"We'll play ball," she repeated, "and then maybe Mom will dig her old bicycle out of the storage room and I'll take you for a ride. And we'll walk. We'll do so much walking together—to the park, to the library to look at those pretty picture books you like so much, to the store and, oh, everywhere.''

Maybe if she loved her child enough and walked far enough, she would be able to forget Spencer and how much she loved him.

At least for today.

He was making everyone crazy, Spencer thought, and yet he just couldn't seem to stop. He must have asked Connor to repeat Kate's last words to him five times already.

She had left him, but before she'd gone, she had tried to play fairy godmother to his brother and grand-mother. She'd done her best to take all the blame for this situation on herself.

"And now I know the answer to the question I've always wondered about. Love hurts just as much as I always thought it would," he said to himself, staring at a photo of Kate someone had taken at his grand-mother's birthday party. "The soul-deep agony that never leaves you."

And yet, he reminded himself, Kate had brought joy to his life, because he couldn't help smiling at the memory of her demanding that he give her the red racket or at his recollection of her description of Fitz, the perfect fiancé. He couldn't forget the sensation of her lips pressed to his, the scent of her hair, the green of her eyes. There was nothing about Kate that he didn't want to remember. The truth was that he mourned her loss deeply, hopelessly, and yet, he didn't want to give up a single memory.

"So does every Fairfield have a soul mate, then?"

he asked himself. He didn't know. He didn't even know if that was what he'd call Kate, but he knew one thing.

What she had brought to his life was something he cherished. He would have regretted never having the chance to know her. The love she'd awakened him to was a rare and wondrous thing. It was not to be missed in this lifetime. And he would have missed it entirely if not for Kate.

And now? What now? What was going on with Kate? Only a day and a half had passed, but already he was worrying. Would she find the security she craved? Was her landlord back to harassing her about Toby already? Would she go looking for love with someone else? And what had caused such a complete change in her attitude toward love?

"Stop killing yourself with questions, Fairfield, because you'll just never know her reasons," he told himself.

But he would always wonder. He and Kate had been engaged twice. Okay, so maybe being engaged at age seven didn't count, but still, neither of them had married. She'd run from love and dreams all her life, but now, suddenly, she wanted love. Had she met someone at his grandmother's party, a man who had touched her heart?

A man unlike himself who had told her that love was the last thing he ever wanted and that she was wise to give up on dreams.

"What was I thinking?" he asked her picture, "when love is the most important thing in the world, and every dream you ever had is precious to me."

He remembered some of those dreams. When she

was small, she'd stood there, hands on hips, and dared him to tell her she couldn't have her heart's desire.

Spencer couldn't help smiling at his vision of a young, proud and defiant Kate.

"She would have a house with a white fence, someday when she grew up," he began haltingly, "and in her yard there would be lots of yellow flowers. She would hang pictures of cats and dogs on her walls." He had to smile at that one. "What else did she say she wanted?" he mused. "Ah yes, a long red dress, a man to call her his heart, two children—one named Cedric," he said, remembering how her jaw had jutted out when she'd said the name, as if daring him to laugh. "And she wanted a real Christmas tree every year."

They were childish desires for the most part, but maybe not so childish for a young girl who had known so little of physical comfort. The fact that she could hold her head high and insist that she would someday have such wonders when her clothes were threadbare and her stomach was often empty had been a mark of her endearing pride.

A child...and a woman should have dreams.

A man should cherish those dreams. And if he was going to ask a woman to marry him, then he should offer her something of value. He should offer her his heart.

Kate had been wise not to stay engaged to a fool who hadn't realized that.

And now he did. What was he going to do?

He shook his head. "Something wild and crazy, sweet Kate. Something loving. If we're going to end it, then we're going to end it on a high note. Something you can relate to your children for the rest of

your life. A tale about the man who once loved you
madly and then set you free.''

Kate came out of the shower and immediately flew
into a panic. Oh no, the doorbell was ringing. Three
quick, impatient rings followed by a pounding.

That usually meant that Toby had been running in
the house. But that couldn't be. She never left him
free to run when she couldn't watch him.

And besides, Toby was across the street at Mrs.
Penway's. Their elderly neighbor had missed Toby so
much that she had begged Kate to let her baby-sit
him this afternoon, and the lady was so lonely and
sweet and generous with her time, her cooking and
her affection for Toby that Kate had been unable to
refuse.

So if Toby wasn't causing the landlord to lose pa-
tience, what was?

"I'm coming," Kate called, throwing on her jeans
and a white T-shirt and hopping to the door as she
tried to get her sneakers on without untying them.

She opened the door, bracing herself for Mr.
Minarri's anger. But the man who stared down at her
wasn't short or paunchy or even angry.

"Hello, angel," he said.

She nearly took a step back. She almost tried to
open her eyes, fearing that she was dreaming. But, of
course, her eyes were already open.

"Spencer." She did her best to keep her voice
steady.

His smile nearly devastated. "How have you been
these past two days?"

Terrible. Miserable. "I've been well." Liar, liar.

"I'm glad." Just two simple words, but his deep

voice seduced her. She wanted to lean against his bare skin and hear that voice rumble through him. She wanted his warm arms around her. Heck, she just wanted him any way she could have him. But, she reminded herself, she'd had him and she'd given him back. She'd left him for his own good, but acknowledging that didn't quell her longing.

Which only meant that she was totally pathetic and needy.

"Spencer, what are you doing here?"

He looked away. For a minute, she thought he wasn't going to answer. "I have a favor to ask of you, Kate. Just one, and yes, I know I've already asked a great deal of you."

She blinked. "I...I'm afraid I don't understand." What she understood was that Spencer was here, and her feelings were so near the surface that she wasn't sure she could control them.

He nodded. "I know. You've gone on with your life. I can't blame you. I admire you for having the courage to end our engagement when it wasn't right for you, when you needed more, but I want to ask you—I'm trying to move in a new direction with my life, too. I've already started making some changes, and I'd like your assistance, your advice on a few things. Would you give me just one more afternoon? Come with me?"

He was trying to move in a new direction and make some changes in his life. What did that mean? Was there a woman involved? "Where?"

"To my house, the place where we first met."

"Oh no." And she almost stepped back. That would be so painful. It had been difficult enough telling him goodbye once. To do it twice?

"You won't recognize it, Kate. I've made some major changes recently. I'd really like you to give me your opinion."

"Oh, I don't know. Your grandmother—"

"Is a wonderful woman, but I don't think she'll understand what I was trying to do with my recent attempts at redecoration. It needs a different kind of woman's eyes. Yours, Kate. I know that this isn't what you want, but your opinion means a great deal to me. Will you come? For yesterday? And so that for just once in our lifetime, we can part with both of our eyes open and maybe even with smiles."

And how could she say no to that when she'd wished the same thing? Her goodbyes with Spencer were always anguished and abrupt.

"Just let me run across to the neighbor and make sure that she doesn't mind watching Toby."

"I'll come with you."

Such a simple statement, but when they entered Mrs. Penway's house, Toby started squealing. He stumbled across the room, both hands raised high in the air.

Spencer swung him high above him, then brought him down and kissed his cheek. He cuddled Toby close. "Missed you lots, big guy."

"Guy," Toby said. The word was almost a sigh, a term of endearment as he reached up to touch Spencer's face. Kate's throat suddenly felt closed up, and she realized just what her son had lost when she'd walked away from Spencer. A father, a wonderful father.

Quietly she explained her situation to Mrs. Penway, who was, of course, delighted to have Toby for a few hours more. And then Spencer was hugging Toby tight and giving him back to Mrs. Penway.

And Kate was on her way to Spencer's house. To give him her opinion, he'd said. And to end things, permanently this time.

She looked out the window the whole way there, afraid that if she turned to him, she would spill her soul and beg him to love her.

For this one last time in her life, she had to be completely practical and ignore her heart's deepest longings.

The first thing Kate saw when they cleared the forested area just outside Spencer's property was a sea of yellow. Daisies and zinnias and roses, other flowers whose names she didn't even know. Yards and yards of them lining the long road leading up to his house.

She sat up higher in the seat. When the car drew to a stop, she stepped out, dazed at the sunny glow of the plants.

"They're so beautiful. Spencer, when did you do this? Your parents had miles of lawns, but no flowers, at least not in front. This lane, it's so perfect."

"It reminds me of you." He moved to stand beside her. "I'm afraid the plants aren't fully settled into their homes just yet. They're freshly planted and still finding their way, but I hoped they'd do."

"I don't understand."

But he didn't answer. Instead, he took her hand, his warm fingers enfolding hers and thrilling her as his touch always did. She tried her best to hide her reaction. Now that she knew her every reaction to him was the result of loving him, she couldn't let him see.

He led her up to the house, a magnificent Georgian

structure with a huge yard, enclosed by a white picket fence.

"The fence is new, too," she said, but Spencer only smiled. He opened the gate and pulled her through. He took her up the stairs and opened the door.

"Your parents always had a butler," she mused.

He smiled. "I let him have the day off. The other servants, too."

So they were alone. Kate swallowed and nodded. She stepped through the door, wondering what he'd done to renovate his house and why he needed her opinion when she had no experience whatsoever with such things.

But only two seconds through the door, her heart started to bang, her chest began to feel tight, and she knew.

Directly across from the entrance, hanging high on the wall, was a painting of an English sheepdog. She looked to the left. Another painting, a cute pair of Siamese cats. And one of a soulful-eyed collie. Another one with three frisky kittens batting a ball of yarn.

All of them were completely out of place in the elegant setting, and a strange choice for a man who had a penchant for Monet.

"Spencer?" she asked, her voice almost breaking. But he placed his hands on her shoulders. He turned her, and what she saw, in the curvature next to the spiraling staircase, was a huge potted Christmas tree in the middle of July.

"What do you think?" he whispered, leaning close.

She swallowed. "I think—" She swallowed again. "Why?"

"To show you that it mattered, that I remembered, that I never ever forgot. Mostly I wanted you to know that I cared. I always cared."

A tear slid slowly down her cheek. She wiped it away.

"Don't cry, sweetheart. I didn't do it to make you cry, but only to show you that I'm sorry for the way things turned out. I should never have tried to muscle you into marrying me. I would never force you to do anything. I just want you to know how much you matter to me, everything about you, all that you ever were and all that you will be.

"I understand why you want to marry for love now, because I realize that I asked you to marry me, because…well, because I *am* a man in love."

Her heart filled up with joy, with disbelief. "Spencer—" she began, but he shook his head.

"Giving you up, Kate, was the hardest thing I've ever done, but I'm grateful for the little time I had with you. I want you to know that. You've changed my life, you've made me come alive and I value you, all of you, the practical side and the fanciful side, too.

"I guess what I'm saying, Kate, is that I don't ever want you to feel that you have to choose a man because life has given you no choices. I'll always love you and even though you can't return that love, I want you to know that I'll always be here for you. You'll always have a rock to lean on, someone who can help you out if you need a friend or a helping hand. Toby will always have a father. And if you ever need someone to spill your dreams to, I'm here. Use me, Kate, until you find the man you're looking for. Don't ever worry about using me. Anything that happens between you and me, no matter the reason, is bound to be good and right. As it always has been.''

Kate's lips trembled, her eyes misted up. She searched for her voice in vain.

"Ah, Kate." And Spencer pulled her to him. He ran his hand soothingly across her hair.

"I don't want to use you," she said, her voice muffled against his shoulder. "And I'm getting your shirt all wet."

His chuckle rumbled through him. "I have another."

She pulled back and dared to look into his gorgeous blue eyes. "You're always doing that, making me feel feminine and soft and...oh, all the things no one else ever made me feel. I don't want to just use you, Spencer, because—"

She looked away. He brought her back with just a touch of his finger. "Tell me."

"I know I didn't make it clear when I left you—I was afraid to tell you the truth—but I had to leave because I was in love with you. I broke the rules. I did the exact opposite of what you asked me to do."

"Oh, Kate," he said on a groan. "You are so wrong. What I wanted—even when I didn't know it—was you. In love with me."

She wasn't quite sure if he was happy about that. He wasn't smiling. She remembered how hard he'd fought against love.

"The Fairfield Curse?" she asked softly.

He shook his head and then he did smile as he took her lips in a gentle kiss. "Oh no, definitely the Fairfield Blessing, my love."

She rose on her toes and kissed him back, lingeringly this time.

"I've been wanting to do that for days," she confessed.

"I've been wanting to do so much more, love. Would you mind very much getting engaged to me again? For the third time. For real this time."

She smiled up at him. "I can't wait to be your wife," she confessed. "I think I've been waiting for you—oh, for years. What took you so long to come back and find me?"

"I guess I just had to find a few things out about myself. Fortunately I had you to help me do that. Now we can make all those dreams we had come true. I seem to recall something about a long red dress and two babies. You wanted one named Cedric?"

She groaned and hid her face against him. "Oh, your memory is much too good."

"I don't think so. I remember loving the feel of you in my arms these past weeks, but the reality is so much better than the memory, Kate."

"Is it?" She moved closer and his arms held her to him. "Yes, it is. I could do this my whole life, Spencer."

"Could you, love? That's good, because I intend to spend many hours this way. And once we're married, I intend to do my best to give Toby another brother or sister."

"Do you think your grandmother and Connor will forgive me for walking out on you?"

"They love you, Kate. *I* love you, Kate. Come here and stop worrying, Kate. My Kate. My love."

And she moved into his arms, where worries didn't matter and where dreams came true.

Epilogue

Spencer gazed around at the guests who had assembled for his grandmother's eighty-first birthday party. It was a larger group than usual. Because of Kate. Now that she had a family again, and she and his grandmother had come to love each other so much, Kate wanted the entire world to celebrate Loretta Fairfield's life.

At that moment, his wife looked up at him and smiled, and his world grew brighter. She started making her way toward him, their two-month-old daughter, Rose, sleeping on her shoulder. He met Kate halfway and bent to kiss her lips.

"Ah, lucky me," he said with a grin. "I've been trying to get your attention all afternoon, love."

She made a face at him and then grinned. "You most certainly have not, because I haven't been able to keep my eyes off you. You've been acting the perfect host, making sure our friends have all that they need, just as you're supposed to. Isn't Dylan and

April's baby, Sam, a little cutie? And Ethan and Maggie's daughter is a complete princess, a tiny miniature of her mother. Motherhood suits Maggie. She absolutely glows, doesn't she?''

"No doubt. I hadn't quite noticed, love," he said, bending to whisper in her ear. "Speaking of glowing, you look beautiful today, Kate."

"You are a flatterer."

"I am a man deeply in love. With my wife." He felt a tugging on his pant leg. "And with my children," he said, looking down at Toby and giving him a wink. "What do you think? Should we escape all this bustle and go build a sand castle later today, big guy?"

Toby's eyes lit up. "Sand castles, Dad," he said. "And beach balls, too. You and me." He beamed back at his father and toddled back to where Dylan's two-and-a-half-year-old half brothers were building roads out of blocks.

"And maybe even later," he told his wife, "we could see if I can make you glow even more. You practically sparkle when you're pregnant, love. And look at all these children. Aren't they wonderful?"

"You know I think they're precious," Kate said. "And you know I can't resist you when you look at me like that. Right now I should be serving canapés or something."

He shook his head. "We pay people to do that."

"Well, then I should be mingling with the guests, making sure they're all happy."

"They're all ecstatic, Kate. Especially my grandmother. What is her current beau's name again? I can't keep track."

Kate wrinkled her nose at him. "Liar. You know

very well his name is William, and he's a sweetheart. He's perfect for Loretta.''

"Is someone talking about me?" Loretta called, turning those knowing blue eyes on her grandson.

"We're always talking about you, Grandmother," Spencer said. "All the time. It's your birthday, after all, and we just want to make sure that you're enjoying it.''

"He's such a liar," she said to Kate. "I know he was trying to sweet-talk his wife. And why wouldn't I be happy, Spencer? My grandchildren are both settled into contented marriages just as I always wanted them to be, aren't they?''

"Blissful marriages, Grandmother," Connor corrected her, pulling Angela closer. His wife gazed up at him adoringly.

"You and Kate are the most wonderful of women, Loretta," Angela said. "You brought me Connor, and love and joy.''

"And a baby on the way, my sweet sister-in-law," Spencer added, gazing down to where Connor's hand had slipped around his wife to rest on her abdomen.

"As if Loretta and I had anything to do with that," Kate said, smiling at Angela. "But things did turn out well, for all of us. Happy birthday, Grandmother." And she moved out of Spencer's arms to give the guest of honor a hug and a chance to hold Rose. "I hope you got everything you wished for.''

"I most certainly did. Look at all these babies and babies on the way. Isn't it wonderful?" she asked as she kissed Rose's fluffy little head.

"Very wonderful," Spencer said as his wife returned to his side. He leaned to whisper in her ear. "I can't wait to have a third child with you, love.''

Kate beamed up at him. "You'd better stop that right now," she whispered back.

"Stop what?"

"Looking at me like that. I just might jump you right here in front of all our guests." Kate kept her voice low, but there was a dare in her eyes.

He grinned. "Might make for an interesting entertainment."

She bopped him on the arm and gave him a quick kiss on the lips. "Later, you," she said.

"Later what?" Loretta demanded.

"Nothing much, Grandmother," Spencer said, with a wicked grin. "Only that my wife is threatening to seduce me. She claims she's going to torture me until I promise to give her another baby."

Kate turned a delicious, endearing shade of pink. "Your grandson is so outrageous, Loretta. Have I told you that lately?"

"Constantly," Loretta said with a laugh, "but you love him, don't you?"

"I adore him," Kate said, gazing up into Spencer's eyes with a quick fire that made him want to carry her out of the room right now. "For a practical woman, I'm embarrassed to admit that he completely takes my breath away. I'm totally helpless and hopeless around him. So, are you happy now that I've confessed my weakness for one of your grandsons, you complete sweetheart?" she asked Loretta.

Loretta shrugged and patted Kate's arm. "Almost happy, dear."

"Only almost?"

"Well, what would make me really happy is more babies."

Kate gave her husband a lusty look. "She's insatiable."

He brushed Kate's lips with his own. "No, love, that would be me."

"Well, that's a relief then," Loretta said. "I think making more children is a perfect idea, the best way to end a perfect birthday. And William and I would love to watch all the babies while all of you go spend some time alone together."

Dylan and Ethan and Connor grew big smiles. Their wives rolled their eyes at them, but smiled back.

"That is, without question, the best idea you've ever had, Grandmother. You're an angel," Spencer told her, kissing his fingers and saluting her.

"I'm a cranky old woman, but I have my good points. Now go on with all of you and leave us two old people to enjoy these little ones. And take your time. Love, after all, takes time." She smiled up at William, who kissed the top of her head. "It's worth waiting for."

And Spencer led his wife to their room. He kicked the door closed. He took Kate into his arms.

"Bless Loretta Fairfield," he said, kissing his wife.

Kate leaned into him, lightly resting her hands on his chest. "She is pretty wonderful, isn't she?"

Spencer chuckled. "I wonder if we'll have to bring a doctor's note to prove that you're pregnant tomorrow."

Kate's eyes widened. "Even Loretta wouldn't be that bold. Besides," she whispered with a smile, "I wouldn't want this unexpected time alone to end too soon. If we're really going to make a baby, we might have to stay up here a while."

Spencer chuckled and lightly kissed Kate's waiting

lips. "A wise woman told us that love takes time, but loving you, my Kate, my heart, will take a lifetime," he whispered as his lips hovered over hers. "Do you suppose we could stop talking so I can kiss you properly, love?"

She rose on her toes, moving nearer. "You always have the most wonderful plans, Spencer," Kate whispered. "Kiss me now. And love me. Make my dreams come true. Again."

And as that was the greatest wish of his heart, he did.

*   *   *   *   *

Coming next month from

SILHOUETTE *Romance*®

Daycare DADS

**She can teach him how to
raise a child,
but what about love...?**

Introducing the amazing new series from

SUSAN MEIER

about single fathers needing to learn the
ABCs of TLC and the special women
up to the challenge.

BABY ON BOARD
January 2003

THE TYCOON'S DOUBLE TROUBLE
March 2003

THE NANNY SOLUTION
May 2003

You won't want to miss a single one!

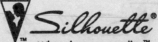

Silhouette®
Where love comes alive™

Silhouette Romance presents tales of
enchanted love and things beyond explanation
in the heartwarming series

Soulmates

Couples destined for each other are brought
together by the powerful magic of love....

Broken hearts are healed
WITH ONE TOUCH
by Karen Rose Smith (on sale January 2003)

Love comes full circle when
CUPID JONES GETS MARRIED
by DeAnna Talcott (on sale February 2003)

Soulmates

Some things are meant to be....

*Available at
your favorite retail outlet.*

Silhouette®
™ *Where love comes alive*™

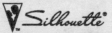

If you enjoyed what you just read,
then we've got an offer you can't resist!

Take 2 bestselling love stories FREE!

Plus get a FREE surprise gift!

SILHOUETTE *Romance*

COMING NEXT MONTH

SRCNM1202